Love Divided

To Tristan

Thanks to Celia Duncan, Ehsan, Hannan,
Brenda and Ruth

First published in Great Britain in 2008
by Piccadilly Press Ltd,
5 Castle Road, London NW1 8PR
www.piccadillypress.co.uk

Text copyright © Vanessa St Clair, 2008

A catalogue record for this book is available from the
British Library

ISBN: 978 1 85340 964 6 (trade paperback)

1 3 5 7 9 10 8 6 4 2

Printed and bound in Great Britain by CPI Bookmarque, Croydon
Typeset by Textype, Cambridge, based on a design by Louise Millar
Cover design by Sue Hellard and Simon Davis
Set in StempelGaramond and Carumba

Vanessa St Clair

Love Stories

Love Divided

Piccadilly Press • London

Chapter 1

♥

Oh God, why oh why did this always have to happen to me? I was walking back from school, minding my own business. At least, I *had* been minding my own business, until I noticed a bunch of kids in front of me, on bikes. They couldn't have been much older than my brother, around ten years old. They'd just dropped all this crap they had been eating – burger wrappers, polystyrene cups – in the middle of the pavement. I hadn't been going to say anything. I mean, normally I'm one of these people who just looks the other way. I'm much too awkward to draw attention to myself. But I'd just been thinking about this boy I used to date and how *awful* he'd been and I was feeling a bit cross. And these kids practically dropped their crapola on my favourite shoes – a drop of Coke splashed right on my leg. Maybe they hadn't realised. Before I could think about it I heard myself say, 'Hey, I'm really sorry, but would you mind picking that stuff up? It's just really dirty, and I've got to walk through it and . . . I've got new shoes on . . .'

I trailed off.

They were looking at me as if I had another head growing from my stomach.

'Oh, it doesn't matter. Sorry.' I wished I hadn't said anything. They had that look about them, like they were trying to think of something to say. And I could bet I knew what it was.

I am an *idiot*!

I've got red hair see, dark red, which around here is enough to mark me out as a freakazoid. Obviously, I don't have a right to say anything to anyone. Added to which, I attract embarrassment, like flies to . . . fly-zappers. I'm a total klutz for one thing. I'm tall for my age and I'm always spilling things or knocking things over. And I have this uncanny ability to attract crazy people. Like, I'm always the one person that the crazy old guy on the bus will sit next to. Not that I mind crazy old guys, I just wish I had the same skill with the young and cute ones.

The kids finally found the power of speech.

'Oi, ginger!'

'Ginger minger!'

'I bet she smells weird!'

'Eeeww, better watch out, she might get really angry!

She might explode!'

Cue crazy laughter. They obviously thought they were being *hilarious* – it's amazing, the self-delusion of some people. And even though it's happened a zillion times before I was still worried I was going to blush, and because I was worried I was going to blush, I could feel myself doing exactly that. My face went bright red, sunburned tomato red, right up to the tips of my ears. Then I couldn't think of a suitably withering response because I was concentrating so hard on keeping my face pointing down at the pavement. If there's anything worse than having red hair, it's the fact that my cheeks go up in flames and everybody can see what I'm feeling. It's like having subtitles over my head: *JUST IN CASE YOU MISSED IT, LUCY BROOKS IS EMBARRASSED.*

I was just bending to pick up the rubbish myself when I heard a voice right behind me. I recognised it, but I couldn't get to the name right away. A boy's voice. Very in control sounding, which was a relief because I was *not* very in control at this point.

'Why don't you get back on your bikes?' the voice said. 'That is, if you know how to ride them. I'm surprised that kids with as few brain cells as you have learned how to balance, actually.'

The chubbier of the boys, who also happened to be

the leader, got this tortured look on his face, like he'd got a stomach ache. But he'd obviously just been having a thought, because then he exclaimed, 'Oi, onion bhaji!' It was Mally – only the coolest boy in school.

'Right,' said Mally. 'Onion bhaji. I don't even know what you mean by that.' Then he paused and pretended to look surprised. 'Oh, you mean I come from a place in which people *eat* onion bhajis. And you know where that is? *England!*' Mally shook his head. 'Go on, why don't you just piss off?'

The chubby boy went, 'Oh!' in a tone that was probably supposed to suggest that he'd still got the upper hand but actually came out like he couldn't think of anything to say. 'C'mon, let's go. This is pointless.'

He was trying to sound tough, but actually he just sounded pathetic.

'Yeah, for once it looks like you've got the right idea,' said Mally.

The others all looked a bit sheepish and couldn't meet my eye. Then they turned around and followed their leader up the street.

Wow, Mally was so damn cool! But then I knew that already. And *I was* a complete idiot. God, this was awkward. Quick, I had to think of something to say!

'What stupid, weren't they . . . I mean losers! Some people have the brain of a gnat.'

'Yeah,' said Mally. 'They were only kids though. Probably it's their parents who are the real losers. It was actually pretty childish of me to resort to their level. It was the first thing that came into my head.'

'I thought it was . . . you were . . . cool!' Nice one Lucy, way to go. First Law of Thermodynamics: never tell a cool person they are cool. It makes you look uncool.

I'd known Mally for ages. Not *known* known, but he'd lived a couple of streets away from me for as long as I could remember. His dad runs the Indian restaurant that everyone goes to and Mally was at the same school as me. His kid brother was even friends with my kid brother; they're both quite nerdy so they got on pretty well. But Mally and I, we'd never really *clicked* before. It might have been his age – he's two years older than me. But it was more likely the fact that I'd found him a bit intimidating. He always seemed to have his iPod clamped to his ears and he dressed quite a lot in black. On top of which, he was really brainy. He was wearing an old black T-shirt now, though I guess it did suit him because it clung in all the right places. His arms were nice too – smooth with just the right amount of muscle, so there was that yummy line on the inside of them when he flexed.

'Anyway,' said Mally. 'I probably should have left those kids to you; I mean I know you can handle yourself, but, well, there was only one of you and four of them.'

'No, I'm glad you got rid of them. It's fine. I mean, *it's* not fine. *I'm* fine. Are you fine?' Oh God. I couldn't stop saying fine!

'I'm fine,' Mally flashed a brief smile at me, which made his cheekbones look even higher ... Oh God, at least he hadn't heard the whole rubbish incident. I'd forgotten all about the rubbish. I couldn't very well *not* pick it up after all this business. But I'd lose any shred of cred by picking it up in front of Mally. But, thinking about it, it was too late for that. If I was standing next to a cool-o-meter, the arrow would be pointing to *COMPLETE AND UTTER LOSER*.

I crouched and picked up a corner of greasy paper by the edges of my fingertips.

'You pick up rubbish? Cool! Weird ... but cool,' said Mally, bending down to help.

Then, *of course*, there wasn't a bin for about twenty miles so we both had to walk down the street holding out pieces of crap in each hand like some kind of rubbish-munching daleks. This was definitely the new Number One on my Most Embarrassing Moments list (and I have *a lot*). This one would be hard to beat.

'Are you going . . .?' I gestured up the street with my head.

'Yeah.'

After about a thousand years we found the bin and let go of our rubbish, then I lost the ability to speak for a bit. Mally must have taken off his headphones without turning his iPod off because I could hear music still coming out of them. It sounded like it was being played by a tiny band in a matchbox.

In desperation I said, 'What . . . what are you listening to?'

'Oh. Umm . . .' Mally fumbled with the wheel and the music stopped. 'The Thrillers. Do you know them?'

'I think I've heard of them. Are they American?'

'Yeah, from the Mid-West or something. I'm not really into them though.'

There was another pause.

'I've just discovered Jeff Buckley,' I said desperately. 'He's amazing. He died – drowned, I think.'

'I know – in the Mississippi River. He *is* amazing. Do you know that song "Hallelujah"?'

'Yes! I bought it on iTunes yesterday! It's so beautiful. It makes my spine tingle. It makes me feel as if I'm the only person in the world who's feeling . . . well . . . who's feeling like that,' I ended lamely. How could I describe my favourite song? It's as if it was written just for me, and the writer knew my innermost thoughts, and it made me feel special and uplifted and a bit melancholy at the same time. But I couldn't say all this because Mally would think I'd gone completely bonkers. I didn't know him *that* well, even if we were managing to have a conversation. Plus we were almost at the door of my house.

'I can't believe you like Jeff Buckley. He's so unusual,' said Mally.

'Oh, and I'm not?' I said. I was *not* flirting because I don't know how to flirt, at least according to Rachel, and to be honest I still felt pretty awkward. It was just the first thing that came out of my mouth.

'No! That's not what I meant. You are. You are very unusual. You pick up other people's rubbish – that's pretty unusual.'

'Oh, so I am a freak. I knew it.' I was laughing now and Mally gave me a great wide grin that illuminated his whole face.

'OK, you're a freak,' he said.

'That's what those boys thought,' I said, embarrassed again. I walked right into that one. Probably Mally *did* actually think I was a freak with my stupid red hair and freckles and tallness. 'Thanks, by the way, for earlier.'

'Oh, no, it's nothing. I like your new haircut.' Mally

was standing there with one finger tucked into his waistband. For one crazy moment I thought he might actually be looking me up and down. My hands shot to my hair. It had been very long and straggly but I'd had it cut to shoulder-length, so on a good day it was tousled. On a bad day it was just a mess. I doubted this was a good day though, so . . . was he taking the piss? But he was just standing there looking at me. I didn't think boys noticed things like haircuts.

'Thanks??' I said idiotically.

'It's a pleasure.' Mally flashed me another smile, put his headphones back in, then he turned on the heels of his beaten-up trainers and was gone.

I shut the front door. I had to call Rachel and tell her what had just happened. I felt like I was going to burst. But Mum got to me first.

'*Loo-cin-dah!*' She is practically the only one who calls me by my full name and she only does that when she's cross.

'Yes?'

Mum poked her head over the stairs. 'I notice the dishwasher hasn't been unloaded even though I asked you to do it this morning. And you need to take your wet clothes out of the washing machine.'

'Sorry, Mum!' Mum had asked me, it was true, but I'd been late and I couldn't decide which tights to wear and I forgot about it. 'Can I please just —'

'No, you can't!'

'But you don't even know what I'm going to say!'

'I don't need to. And don't forget to feed Socks. You know what happened last night.'

'Yes, Mum.' The previous evening I had forgotten to feed Socks and he had started barking really loudly at eleven o'clock. Mum had had to get out of bed and give him some food.

Mum gave a theatrical sigh. 'I know you're sixteen, but really, darling, sometimes you're more like a six-year-old. Before you even think about using the phone, or your computer, can you do your chores?'

Mothers are *so* annoying. I stuck my lip out and flounced into the kitchen.

My little brother, Herbie, was sitting at the kitchen table, bent over his plate and sawing at something with a knife. He looked up when he heard me. 'What's wrong with you?'

'Nothing! Nothing that a pickaxe wouldn't cure anyway.' I bent down and started unloading the dishes noisily. 'What are you doing – or shouldn't I ask?'

'Seeing how many little squares I can make from my sandwich,' said Herbie.

'Right, geek brain.'

'A sandwich is a rectangle, so the number wouldn't be infinite, as it would in a square. My knife is too blunt as well. I've got nine so far.'

I was still full of my encounter with Mally and so desperate to tell Rachel about it I clattered the plates down on the shelves.

'You're going to break those if you carry on like that,' said Herbie.

'Yes, Mini-Mummy,' I said.

Herbie glared at me. I threw the last few into the cupboard and literally ran to my room, dialling Rachel's number as I went.

'Hello? Rach. Guess what just happened to me. You won't believe it!'

When I had finished, I had to hold the phone about a metre away from my ear, Rachel was screaming so hard.

'YOU MUST HAVE DIED!'

'Embarrassing is not the word,' I said.

Rachel has the kind of gorgeous dark brown hair boys come up to admire rather than to mock, and I wondered for a second if she could understand what it felt like to be me. Now she was making vomiting sounds down the phone.

'I mean, I've had to put up with that kind of stuff

before,' I said, a little defensively. 'And by the sounds of it, Mally has too.'

'Yes, I know, sweets, I'm your best friend, remember? The one who's known you for about a million years. Those kids were just jerks. I mean – you must have died when Mally came along. He is *so* cool! And, like, drop-dead gorgeous!'

'He is not! I mean, I can see that he's cute, I suppose. But he's not my type.' As I said it I could feel myself starting to blush – for no reason at all. Luckily we were on the phone and Rachel couldn't see me.

'Not your type?' she said. 'What's not to be your type? He rescued a damsel in distress – that's one major plus over the losers round here. Plus the dreamy eyes,' Rachel put on a sing-song voice. 'The lean muscles. The tousled hair. The strong but mysterious —'

'All right, all right,' I interrupted her. 'He *is* quite cute. I'm not denying that. But I've known him for ages. He's practically the boy next door. Plus, as you well know, I am Officially Off Boys.'

'Apart from DG.'

'Apart from DG.'

Rachel and I were always talking about who we were going to fall in love with, our Dream Guy. He changed every week. His current incarnation was a motorbike-riding lead singer of an Indie rock band who looked like that model in the Hugo Boss ads. We would meet our DG in some totally random but fateful way, like on holiday when he was taking a break from his touring commitments, and had spotted us across a crowded restaurant, and just knew we were The One. Or The Ones, as there were two of us. Though probably, knowing Rachel, she'd get there first. Maybe he could have an identical twin left over for me.

Come to think of it I was getting *way* too into this DG thing.

'But you know, babes, it might be time to let go of the anti-boy thing,' said Rachel. 'I know the Evil Quin was a total jerk, but that was ages ago now.'

'Not ages ago. Three months and three weeks ago.'

I knew exactly how long because the Evil Quin still made me mad. I'd never really fancied him, but he was the first boy to properly ask me out and I was so surprised I'd said yes. He had taken me to the cinema to see a scary film. I HATE scary films, but I think Quin picked it on purpose because in the middle of it, just as the heroine let out a big scream, he snaked his hand along the back of my seat and started pressing my shoulder. I couldn't believe I was living in such a cliché. And then, on the way home, he made a lunge for my lips. And the maddest thing was that because he had paid for my pizza I felt as if I couldn't really stop him.

It was my first proper snog and I'd always thought it might be like something out of James Bond – all soaring music and melting into his manly arms. It wasn't though. It was actually quite boring and uncomfortable.

After that we seemed to be 'an item'. Which seemed to consist of snogging a lot and never actually talking. Which was bad enough, except for one day I felt his hand creeping up my thigh, slowly, like a tarantula. I was wearing a pair of giant pants but that wasn't the reason I was so freaked out. I just didn't want him anywhere near *there*. I wasn't ready! And I'd never *be* ready, at least not with Quin! I leaped out of the car – I could feel myself going the *deepest* red – and started stammering out excuses about having to get home right away to complete some T-shirts I was designing.

I had to finish it – I mean, I should never even have begun it. But it was horrible. I was so obviously crap at this sort of thing that I couldn't tell Quin the truth – I thought I'd hurt him too much. So I said:

'I'm really busy with my T-shirts.'

'My little brother needs help with his homework.' A lie – Herbie *never* needed help with his homework.

And lamest of all, 'My mum says I'm not allowed to hang around with smokers.'

Quin went really quiet and said, 'If you don't like me, just tell me.'

I realise now that I hurt him much more by not being honest. Because Quin was so furious with me he spread it all round school that I was frigid. Mum said to ignore what everyone said, that I had made the right decision. She said 'frigid' was just a word boys used when they were trying to put girls in their place, but it was old-fashioned and had no power any more in the real world. In the end she was right – it all blew over when the gossips found something new to talk about. But the whole episode was enough to put me Officially Off Boys, that's for sure.

'But you know the longer you stay Officially Off Boys, the longer it'll hurt,' said Rachel, at the other end of the phone. 'You need someone to get you in the groove again. What's wrong with Mally? It sounds as if you had a *thing* going on today.'

'If by *thing* you mean a *thing* never to be spoken of again, yes we did. A thing of complete humiliation, of utter —'

'OK, OK, I get your point! Actually you're probably right. You and Mally are quite different.'

'What d'you mean?'

'I mean he's all cool and mysterious, you're a total klutz. And you can be quite loud,' said Rachel.

'You're much louder! Besides, I'm only loud when I'm with my friends! I'm really shy otherwise.'

'I know, I know. And I *am* louder, it's true. That's because I haff to haff vayz off making you do vat I say,' she said.

'If that is meant to be a German accent, it's terrible.'

'Plus you're totally into fashion,' Rachel continued without listening. 'Mally's into saving the world. Mally's the kind of guy who speaks in debates about global warming. B-double-O-ring.'

'I *am* into saving the world, thank you very much. I just wouldn't speak about it in debates. I'd go puce.'

'Anyway, it gives you a chance to see him again.'

'What does?'

'The debate, idiot! It's on Monday. You can see Mally again, your eyes can meet across a crowded room . . .'

'Stop it! We're different, as you said. He obviously saw me and *took pity* on me. Which I suppose is quite nice considering he's so cool, but it definitely is NOT a good beginning to a love story. "Oooh, Lucy, you're so sexy when you get picked on by boys!"'

'Whatever! Maybe on Monday something will happen to change your mind.'

'Yeah, maybe I'll grow a new head by then, but I doubt it,' I said.

Chapter 2

♥

To be honest, I was with Rachel on this one. I thought the debate about global warming was going to be a total waste of time. It's a really important issue, I know, but these school things are usually lame. Apart from it being compulsory, our teacher had also said, *It's for your own good*, which is usually a guarantee it's going to be *bad*, or, at the very least, *boring*.

When we arrived the hall was packed and full of noise. Everyone was mucking about and screeching and elbowing each other. The headmistress had to clap her hands above her head for about a minute before anyone paid her any attention. When she spoke she said that this was the most important issue facing our generation *blah blah blah* and that the motion was: *Global Warming – It's Not My Problem*.

The side that agreed with the motion started first, and fair enough, they did have a tougher argument to win. They said there was no such thing as global warming, that it was some conspiracy to make us all stop doing what we wanted. The planet had always got warmer and colder – look at the last Ice Age. We didn't have to worry about flying abroad on holiday or bother about washing out cat-food tins for recycling. It sounded much easier in fact, and I was halfway to believing they were right.

Then Mally stood up. This time he didn't look at all cool. He looked quite upset. He ran his hand through his hair so that it stood straight up. He didn't sound pompous like the other side had; he spoke quietly, but there was something in his tone that made everyone listen. Then he brought out a trillion facts and figures – the sea-level had risen $X + Y - Z$ amount quicker than natural warming, polar bears in the Arctic were now finding it impossible to hunt and were dying – until we were all completely convinced. His hair kept falling into his eyes and Mally kept giving this little toss of his head that said, *Get out of my way, hair, I've got more important things to worry about, even though you do look impossibly cute falling into my eyes.*

Mally's family was from Bangladesh. His cousin was a schoolteacher who lived in Antarpara, on the bank of a river. But the river kept overflowing. Global warming was melting the ice caps and putting extra water into the sea, which got pushed up into the rivers. His school was flooded and they had nowhere else to go. The crops had failed too because the river was so salty. They were now hungry and homeless. The crisp packets had stopped crinkling in the hall and no one moved. Mally's voice had dropped very low. We were so lucky in England, he said. But it is countries like ours that were causing global warming, while countries like Bangladesh suffered. But just by doing a few simple things – recycling, turning off lights – we could massively benefit people in poorer countries. Global warming, he said, was our problem, and our solution.

When Mally sat down, there was silence for a moment then everyone broke out into crazy applause. 'That was pretty good,' said Rachel in my ear. 'Though Mally did have an advantage.'

'What d'you mean?' I said.

'The whole sob story.'

I poked her hard in the ribs. 'It's not an *advantage*.'

The headmistress hardly had to count up the votes: it was obvious who'd won. Mally – by a mile.

I wanted to go up and tell him how GREAT his speech was, but Mally's hipster friends who were all older than me, had got there first and I didn't feel like pushing through them. Then all these girls from the year above came over and were saying how brilliant he was, and putting their arms around him and standing really close. His mate Raj was there too, looking super-relaxed and jokey. Rachel and I hovered around the edges. I was just about to give up when Mally looked over and saw me.

'Lucy!'

He gave me a massive smile that made the hairs on my arms stand up. I'd had this little speech planned in my head, but now that it came to it, it sounded too cheesy.

'You were great,' I said. Nice one, Lucy, top marks for originality.

'You were amazing,' said Rachel.

'Thanks. It wasn't really me though – my argument was easier to win.' Mally stopped smiling.

'That's what I said!' said Rachel.

'*Rachel!*' I was bright puce.

'Oh, I mean, it's obvious that global warming does exist,' said Rachel. Even she looked a bit awkward now. 'But you did a great job of, ummm, bringing it home.'

'Thanks,' said Mally. 'I think.'

Great. Now he thought my friend and I were total tossers. 'I thought I might do something, maybe, to help?' I said, but before I could say anything else, Raj said to Mally that he'd better make a move, otherwise they'd be late.

'Yeah, OK,' said Mally. 'Look, sorry, Lucy. Raj and I

have to see the Head about our applications to uni. Thanks to Raj here, my timekeeper.'

Raj gave me a big wonky smile. 'The brainbox is only trying to get into Cambridge!'

'Maybe we could speak tomorrow? Or sometime!' said Mally.

'Yes,' I said, over-brightly. 'Sometime!'

Sometime! That was the lamest arrangement ever. I should have at least pinned him down to this week. I just wanted to tell him about an idea I'd had during his speech. I could do something useful that wasn't totally crap (like confronting kids on bikes). I would customise T-shirts. I'd been doing this for ages for friends – just bows and sequins and stuff. But now I could maybe put on a stencil of a polar bear, or a whale. But were whales victims of global warming? I hoped so, then I could make a sequinned spout. But if they were maybe they'd be global-warming winners? More water to swim about in . . .

Hmmm.

This was the kind of thing I needed advice on. I was just so totally clueless. Also I needed a good slogan. *The polar bear needs you! . . .* Hmm. *I'm hot – global warming's not.* A bit confusing. *I'm hot – and so is global warming, but not in a good way.* Hmmmmm.

What else?

What else?

I sat with my fingers poised over my laptop. Long minutes passed.

As I was trying to think, this other voice just tapped away at the back of my brain like a woodpecker. *Why*, tap tap tap, *don't you email Mally* tap tap tap *for advice?*

No! He said *sometime*. He'd think I was pushy.

But you're not after him. It's just for advice.

But still, I shouldn't really email him first. It was up to the boy to email the girl. Also, he'd think I was stupid and trivial – T-shirts!

But you're planning to sell them and donate the proceeds to the school fund. Doesn't that make it un-trivial? Just ask Mally. He's not that serious anyway. He can be quite funny.

He could be quite funny, it was true. Sometimes, when I dropped off my brother at his house, he'd answer the door with a really good impression of Mr Biggs, the science teacher.

Oh God, Mr Biggs had been chair of the debate. I'd had a go at Rachel earlier for being such an *idiot* in front of Mally, but she'd only accused me of sexual tension, which she'd just read about online. Apparently if you had it, you went red in each other's presence and couldn't think of what to say. Basically, she blamed *me* for her being an idiot, said the atmosphere had been tense and she'd just blurted it out, which I thought was a bit of a cheek.

But obviously there had been no *sexual tensity*, or whatever it was called. Mally had been surrounded by other girls and he hadn't even been looking at me, until right at the end.

Which was why, I thought with a little stab of excitement, I *could* email him. We obviously didn't fancy each other so there was no way my email could be misinterpreted. It would just be as one . . . activist . . . to another.

Right.

I could email his school address – we all had one in the same format for when the school wanted to get hold of us (no escape from the evil eye). Just a quick note and then I could get on with the design of the T-shirts.

What should I say?

From: Loocee@blueyonder.co.uk
To: m.khan@stmarys.co.uk
Subject: Hi!

I deleted the exclamation mark. Too keen.

Subject: Hi.
Hi Mally,
Just thought I'd write a quick note to say how great
I thought you were today.

I'd already told him I thought he was great. God, I was boring! Plus, 'great' – it was like saying 'nice'. I took out 'great' and put in 'brilliant'.

Hi Mally,
Just thought I'd write a quick note to say how brilliant I thought you were today.
What you said was amazing.

I wanted to write that I'd known about global warming before, in a vague way. It was the reason Mum went to the local farmers' market, when she could afford it, so the vegetables didn't have to be driven as far. But I hadn't actually *understood* it before now. The people in countries like Bangladesh had seemed so far away, but Mally's speech had made me realise they were just like us.

I didn't write any of this down. I tried to, but it sounded too cheesy, so I deleted it all.

After literally an hour, this is what I came up with:

Love Divided

Hi Mally,

Just thought I'd write a quick note to say how brilliant I thought you were today. What you said was amazing, you really made me think. I thought I'd make some T-shirts about global warming. Is it OK to run some things by you?

Thanks,

Lucy

I wasn't that pleased with it – I sounded pretty lame. But I hit *send* anyway and then surfed the web for a while. I wanted to be online in case Mally emailed me back.

But one hour later, Mally had *not* emailed me back! My eyes hurt. Better go and have dinner.

One hour forty-three minutes later, Mally still had not emailed me back! I didn't really know what to do. Watch TV I supposed.

... OhmyGod, three hours ten minutes later and Mally *still* had not emailed me back. I knew the precise time because I was checking it at the top of my screen every three seconds. I kept thinking that three hours wasn't such a long time to wait for a reply. He might have gone out. He might have a life! Then again, it was a school night and it was the evening and ... oh Jeez, I was so *humiliated*! *Why* had I had to bother him with my stupid stupid T-shirt idea? He obviously thought it was not even worth replying. I was a total fool. Mally was far too cool for me. Who did I think I was?

OK, OK, during the last three hours fifty-five minutes and twenty-four seconds, I had been forced to admit it. I did like him. Just a little bit.

I'd got no chance though.

I hit *sleep* on my computer. Then I remembered I should turn it off. I might have lost the boy but I didn't have to lose the planet too.

In the morning there was still no email. I checked it as soon as I woke up, even though I had to admit it was quite unlikely Mally would have sent one in the middle of the night. Then I had to go into school, and of course, as soon as I walked in, there he was. Mally was at the top of the stairs and I was at the bottom, but luckily I spotted him before he saw me. My heart gave a giant lurch and I spun round on my heel, bumping into some Year Sevens in my eagerness to get out. I had to skulk around in the yard until the bell rang, pretending to all my friends that I had a really important text to send.

I skipped lunch and ate three packets of Twiglets instead. Not so good for my diet – not that I was on a diet, I just wouldn't mind losing some weight, just a couple of pounds. Mum said I was mad, but I felt too big, especially compared to the girls I saw in magazines. But even breaking my non-diet diet was better than risking the utter humiliation of bumping into Mally.

Rachel could see immediately that something was wrong and she didn't launch into her usual mad routine. When I told her I had sent an email to Mally but hadn't got a reply, even this morning, a whole thirteen and a half hours later, she put her arm round me.

'You like him, don't you?'

'Yeah, OK, I admit it. You were right. But now I've completely blown it, oh God, and it's sooooo embarrassing.'

'Sweetie! His email might not be working,' said Rachel.

'I've thought of that. About a thousand times. But whenever someone doesn't reply that's what I always think, and they've always got it, they've just been really slow at answering.'

'I don't know . . .'

'It's far more likely that he just doesn't want to answer.'

Rachel squeezed my shoulder. 'Then he's an idiot.'

'Yeah, an idiot,' I said. But what I really thought was

that he was probably pretty smart, not wanting to be involved with me. Awkward, blushing, litter-picking-up me. Why would someone like Mally be interested? 'I've scared him off, haven't I, by emailing?'

'But he doesn't know that you like him. He just thinks you're a friend at this point. And if one of your friends didn't answer straight away, you wouldn't be upset, would you?' said Rachel.

'Great. I'm a friend. That's just what I need.'

'I didn't say that! But . . .'

'What?' I said.

'Well, have you thought that maybe you just *think* you like him because you think he doesn't like you?' she said.

It was true that I hadn't admitted to myself how much I fancied Mally. But I had liked him even *before* I sent him the email. If I was honest, that was *why* I had sent him the email. 'I don't think so,' I said. 'I like Mally because he's so different from the rest of the boys round here. Most of them are so full of front.'

'Tell me about it,' said Rachel. 'Though sometimes *some* front is . . . a tiny bit sexy, right?'

'Not to me,' I said.

'No, you're right,' said Rachel.

'I thought Mally was full of front. Until he rescued me and helped me pick up rubbish! Though he did tell those kids where to go. But that wasn't front, exactly. Then, you know, the debate, he was just so, so passionate and not cool at all . . .' I trailed off.

'You should have asked my advice!' said Rachel. 'I'm the expert when it comes to boys! Seriously though, hon, it's not all bad. At least you can be friends with him now you've got to know him a bit. You can hang out with your brothers as a foursome.'

I pulled a face. 'A foursome! You mean, me and three boys, one of whom is my *brother*?'

Rachel and I burst out laughing.

'OH MY GOD!' said Rachel. 'Don't take me there! That would have to be the least appetising foursome in history.'

My mind kept wandering all through afternoon lessons. My brain was completely trying to do me in, because it *kept on* turning to Mally, even though he was the last thing I actually wanted to think about.

Here's what my brain sounded like: *Do you think Mally saw me on the stairs? Then he would have seen me running away and –* STOP! *Think about something else. Hmmm, OK, looks like spring is finally arriving. Leaves on trees at last, ice-creams! Swimming. Bikini shame! Bet Mally'd look pretty cute in a pair of –* STOP IT.

Chemistry, chemistry, periodic table; what is technetium anyway? Sounds like the name of an online super geek. Oh God, why did I have to send Mally that email? STOP IT STOP IT, PLEASE STOP IT.

I was quite depressed by the time school ended, and utterly sick of myself. Rachel wanted to walk back with me, but I said I'd be OK. I just felt like going home and watching TV.

I was heading out of the playground when I saw Mally and Raj loitering around the school gates, as if they were waiting for someone. Oh blimey, now I had no protection! But if they were waiting for someone, why were they walking over to me? There was absolutely nothing I could do to escape. Most of the other kids had gone home. It was just Mally, his mate and me and a giant expanse of concrete.

I hoped it would be over quickly.

'Howya doing, Lucy?' said Raj, with his trademark cheeky grin.

'Fine, thanks,' I mumbled, looking down at the ground. Raj was wearing a giant pair of old school trainers, not the sort you could get in shops round Redworth.

'Cool. OK, catch ya later, yeah, bro?' he said to Mally, with a wink.

Now it was just Mally and me.

'I'm sorry I didn't get to talk to you after the debate,' said Mally after a silence. 'I felt like I was a bit rude.'

Why was he apologising about that? He probably felt sorry for me. 'It's OK, it's fine,' I said. I was blushing right up to the roots of my hair and I had to drop my head down and pretend to be looking for something in my bag. Why wouldn't he just go *away*?

'I think you said you wanted to do something, I dunno, to help? After the debate. Maybe I didn't hear you properly.'

Oh bloody hell. I was boiling over with confusion. What about the email? I didn't know what else to say, so I just said, 'Yesss,' as if I was thinking loads of deep thoughts.

'I mean, you don't have to!' said Mally. 'I'm not pushing you. I just, I just wanted to apologise, I guess.' He stopped and thrust his hands into his trouser pockets.

'I was thinking about T-shirts,' I said. 'Did you . . . get my email?'

'Email? No. When did you send it?'

NO!!!

'Oh, around seven,' . . . thirty-six, I added silently.

'I wasn't online after six yesterday. I had a tonne of maths homework. What did it say?'

HE HADN'T GOT IT!

'Oh, it was no big deal,' I said. 'I just thought I might make some T-shirts for the school fund. I've made them before, just silly ones, but I thought I'd make some for global warming.'

'That's a great idea,' Mally said. Then he gave me a smile that made my skin goosebump. 'I was kind of hoping you might email me actually.'

He *was*? I flushed up to the roots of my hair. Bloody hell, Lucy, stop being so awkward!

'Really?' I said, only my voice came out all weird and wobbly.

'Yeah, really,' he said, with the same slow smile. 'I was going to text you, only, if you can believe it, I don't have your number.'

'Oh.' I stood there, rooted to the spot, but staring and staring at him with a feeling of incredible excitement.

'I was going to ask you if you wanted to meet up tomorrow afternoon. We could talk about your T-shirt idea then, if you like.'

'Yes! I'd love to. Only . . .' Oh *no*! *I'd forgotten about Socks!* '. . . Only on Saturday afternoon I have to take the dog for a walk. It was kind of a bargain my mum and I made when we got him.' God, I sounded lame.

'That sounds great,' said Mally, turning towards the school gates and giving his hair a little shake. 'If that's OK?'

He really was impossibly cute.

'Really? You want to come on a *dog walk*?'

'Why not? The weather is just getting good, and if that's what you're doing, I'm in.'

OHMYGOD. I'd just made a date with Mally. If you could call a dog walk a date. Which I could and I would!!!

When we reached my house we stood awkwardly, looking at each other.

'OK then, Lou-ceee . . .' said Mally.

Just the way he pronounced my name, long and slow, gave me the shivers.

'OK then, Mally.'

'I'll see you tomorrow.'

Mally arrived early. I knew because I was still upstairs applying mascara and the doorbell gave me a shock and I smudged it on to my eyebrow. Then I heard his footsteps in the hall and the sound of muffled voices. After a moment I heard my mum laughing. Lordy, what was he saying to her? I had to get down there.

I still wasn't happy with my outfit – I hadn't wanted to look as if I'd worked too hard – no high heels; but I'd also wanted to wear something that didn't make me look fat, so no baggy pair of old cords. Which left . . . not that much really. I finally settled for my favourite jeans with a pale green cotton tunic top. For once I didn't mind my hair or my pale skin – the colour of the tunic seemed to suit them. I fluffed my hands through my hair – aiming for tousled – then I rubbed off the mascara. It would have to do.

I ran downstairs.

I was in such a hurry that I collided with the doorway on my way in but I pretended it didn't hurt. And *there* was real-life Mally in *my* kitchen, leaning on the table, with one long leg bent up against the table leg, waiting for me.

The kitchen suddenly seemed much too small.

Mum smiled. 'Ah Lucy. Mally was just telling me you're going for a walk.'

I hadn't wanted Mum to know Mally coming over was a big deal, just in case it wasn't. I loved my mum and everything but I know what she's like. She'd be full of questions and then she'd say something really embarrassing like, *Where are you going on your date?* And then she'd probably ask me if I'd finished all my homework, or hassle me about something I'd forgotten to do. I know I can be scatty, but at the same time Mum can be quite bossy and go on at me a lot.

So to avoid mother-shame, I had said something vague about Mally coming round to take Socks out because he was helping me with something for school. Mum had had some work she'd brought home for the weekend and she was screwing up her eyes at it when I told her, so she just nodded.

'Socks!' said Mally, rubbing his neck. 'Good to see you again!' Socks was in heaven, pressing himself against Mally's legs. I knew exactly how he felt.

He looked up. 'Hi Lucy.' My heart skipped a beat. He was wearing a great pair of jeans, not too baggy, not too tight. His legs looked very sexy and I could see the perfect brown skin of his hip bone above his waistband. His retro trainers and beaten-up navy blue coat looked old, but not at all grotty. Mally caught me looking him up and down and winked at me, in a really *naughty* way that gave my heart a little electric shock. The kitchen was growing tinier and tinier until I felt as if my head might explode.

I had to get out of there.

'We should probably go!' I said, a bit breathlessly.

'Well, have fun,' said Mum. 'Are you sure you're going to be warm enough? It's quite cold outside.'

'Yes, Mum! The sun's out.'

Mum looked doubtful, but before she could grab my arms and manhandle me into a coat I sped out of the front door.

* * *

I loved taking Socks down by the river. Down there you'd never know that a huge bustling town was just around the corner. For a start you couldn't hear anything but water whooshing by. You couldn't see many houses at all through the trees, and the banks were covered with daffodils. Daffodils are great, they mean summer is just around the corner. Though it wasn't that hot today; Mum might have been right about the weather. Still, it smelled lovely, damp and fresh.

I let Socks off the lead and he scampered about, shoving his nose in clumps of grass. I suddenly felt incredibly happy. It was spring and I had the cutest boy in school walking next to me.

'So,' said Mally. 'You wanted to ask me about T-shirts?'

'Oh – yeah! Well, I thought I would put an animal on the front, one that was threatened by global warming, and then a tag line. Only, when I thought about it more, I wasn't absolutely sure which animals were in trouble. The polar bear, of course, but is the whale, or the dolphin?'

'Loads of them are but the polar bear is probably your best bet,' said Mally. 'It's the most instantly recognisable in terms of global warming.'

'Right. But all the tag lines I thought of are incredibly cheesy. Like, *It's hot, I'm not. It's hot, and so am I.*'

Mally burst out laughing. 'That's actually pretty good. I can see that last one on you.'

'Can you?' I said, raising my eyes to meet his, for once. I couldn't believe I wasn't blushing.

We talked some more about ideas and different things I could do and I found myself having new ideas on the spot. Mally didn't mock me or say they were crap. He actually seemed to be listening to me.

'How about *Global warming is not cool*?' I said. 'Short and to the point.'

'That sounds perfect!' said Mally, smiling at me. 'You're not just a pretty face. Though you *are* pretty, that's for sure. Gorgeous, in fact.'

I didn't know what to say, so we just stared at each other, smiling, our eyes drawn together like magnets. I kept thinking, *I can't believe this is actually happening*. None of my fantasies had ever matched up to this. And we'd probably still be standing there locked together if Socks hadn't started barking and I'd finally had to look away.

'Socks!! Come back! Sorry, he loves chasing squirrels.'

'I don't blame him. If I was a dog, that's what I'd like too,' said Mally.

'Do you know that dogs have a sense of humour? They've recorded these really high-pitched sounds dogs make when they're playing; it's like laughter.'

'Really?' said Mally, taking my hand in his. 'I'm sure it's true. I always think the next-door neighbour's dog is laughing at me when I go to school in the morning. He's just so perky, and I'm just so . . . not.'

I was trying to keep on being normal even though I could feel Mally's hand burning through my skin. I couldn't believe that Mally ever looked anything less than gorgeous, even first thing. He looked gorgeous now. He had the most ridiculously long eyelashes. And the most perfectly formed nose.

'You know, you have a nose Michael Jackson would kill for.' It was my turn to flirt – very unlike me, but this whole thing was very unlike me, and it felt *great*.

'I'm glad you like it,' said Mally. 'It cost me almost as much as it cost him.'

'Really? You mean you've had . . .' I realised he was joking. 'You mean, I'm on a date with a rich man?'

Mally's face broke out into a grin. 'Imagine if I told my dad I was getting plastic surgery. Oh no, Maladhar,' he said in his dad's voice, 'don't be like the Big Brother. I didn't come to England for this!'

He really was pretty good at voices. I didn't dare ask him to do me.

'When did your parents come over here?' I asked. It was crazy that I'd known Mally all these years but actually I didn't really *know* anything about him.

'They came in the Seventies. Lots of Bangladeshis came then. In search of a better life and all that. Initially they lived in London; my cousins have a flat there. But they didn't like it – they wanted a safer place to bring up us kids. Then my dad heard about the restaurant here and even though he'd never run a restaurant before – he didn't even know how to cook – he decided to move us all out to Redworth.'

'Wow, pretty brave,' I said.

'Yeah. Mad, some might say!'

I knew Mr Khan's restaurant. It was on the High Street and it was always bustling. 'But Khan's is really successful.'

'Dad works hard. When we were kids he used to work fourteen-hour days. That's not even unusual when you've come from rural Bangladesh. I guess we all understand the value of hard work. Tareque's at Cambridge University, where I intend to go. Dad wants to give us what he never had growing up. Nice house, nice car, all that stuff.'

I was impressed. I'd always thought the value of hard work was, I don't know, about 15p. I preferred to take it easy. 'But your dad has already given you what he never had; your house is really nice.'

'Yeah.'

'Gravel drive! Very posh. We can only manage crazy paving. And a cat statue.'

'I noticed that. What is that?'

'You mean, *who* is that?' I said, mock-angry. '*That* is Cheshire. Dad found him on his travels. Needed a good home, he said. Though I think he was pretty heavy to bring back in his suitcase.'

'I can imagine. He must really like cats.'

'He did. I always liked dogs more. But Dad said cats were less effort, more independent. He said dogs were too desperate.'

'My parents don't like dogs either. In Bangladesh dogs carry disease. Even though I've told them a million times it's different over here, they still don't get it. I love dogs.' Mally bent down and scooped up Socks, planting a big loud kiss on the top of his head.

'Mum got Socks for me just before she and Dad split up. He's grown up with me, haven't you, Socks?' I ruffled his grey muzzle. 'He's a rescue dog though, so he wasn't a puppy when we got him. He's probably pretty old now.'

'Old dogs are the best. They're like wise old men,' said Mally, straightening up. 'Do you still get to see your dad a lot?'

'Not so much. My dad is completely different from your dad. Even when he was married to Mum he wasn't around. I mean, not properly.'

My voice had dropped and I saw that Mally was looking at me.

'I'm sorry,' he said, really gently.

'It's OK. He used to drink too much, when he was with us, so when Mum kicked him out it was a bit of a relief. Then he stopped, and then he found a new wife. I've only met her once, so I don't see him so much, no.'

'That must be tough,' said Mally. He squeezed my hand.

I really don't mind that Dad doesn't make the effort to see Herbie and me very often – at least I tell myself I don't mind. But now, with Mally right beside me, I suddenly found myself blinking back tears.

'It is tough, yeah.'

I couldn't believe I was telling him about my dad – I hardly knew him. But somehow it seemed OK; I felt safe with him, as if I could tell him anything.

'I can't imagine anyone not choosing to see you as often as they could,' said Mally, bumping me gently with his shoulder. 'I know I would.'

I blushed. Then I remembered that Mally had lived a couple of streets away practically our whole lives and we'd barely exchanged more than a few words. I said this to him.

'Yeah,' said Mally, 'but for most of those years I was just a child. I always thought you were pretty, but it wasn't until that afternoon with those stupid kids that I realised how truly gorgeous you are.'

Gorgeous; that word again! But hold on a minute. 'Why on that embarrassing afternoon, of all days?' I asked him.

'Because you looked so, so . . . vulnerable. Not that I only like vulnerable women! But before that I always thought you were a bit of a . . . fashion vixen . . . I guess.'

'*Fashion vixen?* That's how I used to think of you! I mean, not the fashion part.'

'Or the vixen part hopefully,' said Mally, laughing. 'More a fox. Or a wolf?'

'Yeah!' I laughed. 'No, more a . . . cool, umm, cat.'

Mally laughed. 'Really?'

'Too cool for school. I was a bit in awe of you,' I said.

'But I was a bit in awe of *you*! That's why I never stuck around your house for long.'

How *anyone* could be in awe of me I couldn't imagine. Boys were often scared of Rachel, especially when she was being loud. But not me.

We smiled at each other.

'Is that why you said, "See you sometime," when I came up to you after the debate?' I said.

Mally cringed. 'I kept thinking about that. That was so utterly lame. But I didn't want to sound too keen.'

'You know, when I sent you that email, I obsessed about it all night, waiting for you to answer.'

Mally stopped walking and pulled me towards him. I could feel the buttons of his coat pressing through my tunic. I shivered.

'Are you cold?'

'No. I mean, maybe.' But I wasn't shivering because of the cold.

'Here, take my scarf.'

Mally unwound it and hooped it round the back of both our necks. Then he wrapped his arms tightly round me. He smelled good, of lemons and soap and that warm boy smell, as if he'd been running. His arms felt tight around my back.

'I'm glad,' he said.

'Glad?'

'Glad you obsessed all night. I can't believe someone as beautiful as you would do that over me, but I'm glad.'

I wanted to tell him I wasn't beautiful – had he seen my

thighs? But it was good that he thought it, and at that moment I almost believed him, staring into his eyes.

'I didn't obsess *all* night,' I teased. 'I did manage to get some sleep. Not much, but some.'

'Good. Because I was up. I should have been working, but instead I was thinking about you.'

'Really?'

'Mmmhmm.'

I was finding the conversation increasingly hard to concentrate on, what with Mally's lips centimetres from mine.

Kiss me, please kiss me, I thought. He was just too close, my heart was racing.

Then he kissed me.

Mmmm, warmth and softness and this incredible tingling sensation right up to my scalp.

I wished we could stay like that for ever.

But the next thing I knew, Socks was scrabbling at my leg with his muddy paws and we broke apart, flushed and laughing.

'I think he's jealous,' said Mally.

'He should be,' I said. 'He's got competition now.'

Mally smiled. 'Really? I'm honoured.'

'Good,' I said softly. Then Mally put a hand on either side of my face and brought my lips to his again and kissed me harder. This time the world spun around and around until I was about to pass out.

When I opened my eyes again I knew everything would be different.

chapter 3

♥

Pretty soon after Mally and I started seeing each other it was the Easter holidays, which meant we could spend the whole day together. Yes, that's right, Mally and I were *seeing each other.* Seeing each other every day, all day in fact, and I was so happy I was walking on air. People always say, 'I was walking on air', but up until then I hadn't known what they'd actually meant. Shiny bubbles of happiness were bouncing around inside my chest and I wouldn't have been surprised if I'd looked down one day and seen the whole of Redworth spread out beneath my feet.

Mally was the most perfect boyfriend I could ever have dreamed of. Every day he'd do something romantic, like pick me a bunch of wild flowers, or leave me a sweet message in my coat pocket, or text me a dirty joke. OK, so the last one wasn't exactly romantic, but it made me laugh. When we were together I couldn't keep my hands off him; I always wanted to sit on his knee, or kiss his face, and he seemed to want to do the same. Now I knew where another cliché came from too – 'joined at the hip'. Or in our case, the lips. Did I mention that we kissed? Well we did, *a lot*, and every one of them made butterflies to go with the bubbles until I could hardly feel the ground at all.

At night, when we had to go back to our separate houses, I lay in my bedroom with the phone pressed between the pillow and my ear, talking to Mally for hours. We had only just said goodbye to each other, so we didn't have anything new to say, but it didn't matter. We talked about *everything*, and it was just so amazing to have found someone who listened to me, who got me totally, and who on top of all that was so incredibly sexy.

One evening Mally mentioned that his family were having a get-together on Sunday at his house and asked me if I'd like to come. Would I ever! Mally had told me so much about his family, I couldn't wait to meet them. His brother Tareque would be down from Cambridge and his cousins from London. It was no big deal, he said, but it was to me.

I spent hours deciding what to wear – I didn't want to look too smart but at the same time I didn't know if everyone else was going to be dressed up. Would they be wearing saris? Or full headscarves? God, would I stick out like a sore thumb?

In the event everyone was really nice to me. We all sat around a big table in the dining room (Mally's house actually had a dining room!) with everyone talking over everyone else and reaching across and helping themselves to enormous silver dishes of different coloured food. It all smelled incredible. I'd never even seen some of them before. There was so much noise and action that it didn't matter that I sat next to Mally not saying much. Mally's mum never seemed to sit down; she was wearing a headscarf that covered her hair, even though Mally's aunt was not, and she was constantly in and out of the kitchen, taking away empty plates and bringing new ones in. I wondered if Mr Khan would help her, but he never seemed to. He was too busy talking.

Even though it was Sunday Mr Khan still looked very smart. He was sitting very upright in a suit, and his hair looked as if it had been sculpted from wood. I was a little in awe of him and I was dreading him asking me any questions. When he spoke he addressed the whole table as if he were a public speaker, and everyone else fell silent. He seemed pretty impenetrable, but I noticed that when he looked at his kids his face broke into a huge smile. Now I knew where Mally's smile came from.

'Tareque,' he said, beaming, 'has joined the

University Law Society, have you not, Tareque?'

'Dad, I'm sure they don't want to know all my business,' said Tareque.

'Oh, don't worry – we know all about your business already! Your father makes sure of that!' said Aunt Shefali. I liked Aunt Shefali; her eyes twinkled when she spoke and she had a way of making us all part of some kind of conspiracy.

'But do you know about Tareque's society, eh? You'll soon be head of it, yes, Tareque?' said Mr Khan.

'Dad! Let's not get ahead of ourselves! I've only just joined.' Tareque smiled and looked down at his plate.

'Ah, but Tareque always gets made the leader. Do you remember at school, you'd only just joined the Law Society there, and you were made head?'

'Dad, that's slightly different. There were only three people in the Law Society at school. It was hardly an achievement.'

'Getting into Cambridge is an achievement! First of your school to have done so,' said Mr Khan.

'I don't know about that, Dad.' Tareque was older and shorter than Mally, with a neat side parting. I could totally imagine him as head of the Law Society, but he wasn't like one of those flashy lawyers on TV. He was very still and calm and when we'd been introduced he had taken my hand and shaken it, as if he was about forty years old. He seemed nice though.

Uncle Rafiq laughed. 'Ah Tareque, you are too modest. But that's a good thing too, is it not? And you, Mally, I hear you were a winner too, eh, in your school debate?'

I was beginning to feel like a serious loser. I hadn't done anything recently except . . . fall in love. A slow smile immediately crept across my face, which I hid behind my napkin. *Except fall in love?* But falling in love was the most amazing thing I could ever do!

The conversation had turned to Mally and the debate, and they were asking him what else he planned to do. Meanwhile Aunt Shefali looked at me.

'Lucy, you are at school with Mally, is that right?'

Oh God, I was going to have to speak. I felt myself grow hot. 'Umm, yes, different year though.'

'Ah, so you don't spend too much time together,' she said.

'Oh yes, we do. We spend quite a lot of time together.' I smiled at Mally, who smiled back.

'I see. So, you are good friends?'

It was on the tip of my tongue to say, we're more than good friends, but I held back. I didn't know what Mally had said to his parents. I mean, it was pretty obvious that something was going on; my mum had guessed it straight away, as soon as I'd come home wearing a massive grin. But Mally's family might be different.

'Lucy lives a few streets away,' said Mr Khan. 'Ehsan is friends with her brother. She is a neighbour.' He gave me a short smile.

Then the conversation moved on to Ehsan, and what genius things he'd been doing at school and the whole thing would normally have bugged the hell out of me if it had been any one else's family. But Aunt Shefali kept asking her questions in such a teasing way, and Mr Khan was so pleased that it didn't seem so much like boasting, but more like a good kind of pride. I wished my dad would be half as proud of me.

Mally's cousins were there too: Huseyn, who looked about fifteen, and his two younger sisters, Leena and Nanda. Neither of the girls said a word through the whole of lunch, except to answer questions about school. I couldn't believe how well mannered they were compared to most kids their age.

I had eaten a tonne of food. I could feel Mally's leg pressing against mine under the table and I reached under and squeezed it. Even though Mally's family was completely different from mine and I hadn't said much, I felt happy and relaxed because Mally and I were together and it was the best thing that had ever happened to me.

Nothing could touch me.

'And how about Cousin Nina?' Mally, who had obviously been following the conversation better than me, asked.

'She's very well,' said Aunt Shefali. 'She's enjoying life.'

Her husband snorted. 'Enjoying life, yes, you could put it like that!'

'Come come Rafiq, we are in England now. She's bound to do what the English do. She *is* a student after all.'

'Why, what is it?' said Mr Khan.

'She is dating someone, Father, that is all,' said Tareque.

'Someone? Who?' said Mr Khan, his eyebrows almost in his hairline.

'I believe he is very nice. Martin someone-or-other.'

'Martin someone-or-other? An English boy then. Do her parents know?'

'Oh yes, they know,' said Uncle Rafiq. 'She had this Martin to stay with her – in their own house.'

'They are fine with it. And why should they not be?' said Aunt Shefali.

'He is a nice boy,' said Uncle Rafiq, pulling a face that might have been either a grimace or a smile.

'Exactly!' said Aunt Shefali.

Then Uncle Rafiq and Mr Khan started talking together in a language that had to be Bengali and everyone looked embarrassed. I had a feeling I was missing something. But then they switched to English again and I was too full and happy to think about it properly.

After a while it started to grow darker outside. I looked at my watch. Blimey, I'd been at Mally's house for hours! I'd better go. The rest of Mally's family didn't look like moving for a while.

I stood up a bit awkwardly, my chair scraping on the wooden floor. 'Well, I'd better go, I think. Thank you so much for having me!'

Everyone's faces turned towards me and I started to blush. But then Mrs Khan spoke; it was the first thing she'd said to me all day.

'Thank you very much for coming, Lucy. It has been a pleasure to meet you,' she said, bowing her head. 'It is always good to meet one of Maladhar's friends.'

'Great to meet you too, thank you, it was all so delicious.' I smiled at Mally's mother and gave a vague wave to everyone else.

'I'll see you out,' said Mally.

* * *

As soon as we were out of the door Mally pulled me towards him. I giggled.

'Careful, your parents might see us.'

'They won't,' said Mally, gesturing behind us. The porch was made from thick coloured glass. I guess he was right – no one could see anything through there.

'Do you not want them to see us?' I said, teasing.

'I don't care. Come here!'

His arms felt so strong and warm around my waist and his lips still tasted faintly of the pudding we'd had.

'Mmm, that reminds me,' I said, between kisses. 'What did we eat in there? It was delicious.'

'There were loads of things. Mughlai lamb biriani. Naan, alu-jira. The minced chicken was reshmi kebab. What else, there was a lamb kalia and for pudding there was Bangladeshi egg haloa and some shemai. Mum really went to town.'

'Wow. I don't think I've had any of those things in a restaurant. It must have taken her hours.'

'Yeah, she started days ago. Dad doesn't cook in the house.'

'My mum isn't a bad cook. But she usually doesn't start a meal more than an hour before we're going to eat. Why don't you come over?'

'I'd love to.'

Love Divided

We decided Mally would come next Sunday. Then he could get to know my mum too and we'd be fully introduced to each other's families like real-life grown-ups.

'Perfect. But I'll see you tomorrow?' said Mally, looking at me from under his adorable floppy fringe.

'Try and keep me away. And by the way, thanks. I loved today, meeting your family. Thanks for asking me.'

'Thanks for coming. You weren't too bored though? You seemed a bit quiet.'

'Bored? No! I was just a bit ... shy ... that's all.'

'I don't know what you've got to be shy about. You have so many talents,' said Mally, kissing me all over my face. 'You're multi-faceted.' I imagined 'multi-faceted' must be something good, from the way he was nibbling on my earlobes. I'd have to Google it when I got home.

'You're sure you don't want me to walk you back?' Mally said.

'I'll be fine. You should go in.' It was ridiculous the way I hated leaving him, even if it was just to go to sleep. But I could still feel his teeth marks on my ears and his lip prints on my nose as I walked off down the street, and that helped. It helped a lot.

Chapter 4

♥

I met Mally in the hall of my house and gave him the biggest kiss ever. Well, maybe not the *biggest* kiss ever. Herbie and Mum were in the sitting room and I didn't want to be in full snog with them basically just two metres away.

'Come through,' I said.

'Oh, hello again, Mally.' Mum stood up and smoothed down her skirt.

Herbie was lying on the floor playing on his Xbox. He was surrounded by all kinds of crap – empty crisp packets, abandoned comic books, smelly trainers. Even if he *was* a nerd, he still had a rubbish-making super-power, just like every other ten-year-old.

'Herbie!' Mum said sharply. 'Get up, please!'

Herbie pushed his glasses further up his nose and twisted round. 'Oh hi, Mally. Have you come as Lucy's date?'

'Herbie, do you have to?' I said.

'Yes, I have come as Lucy's date,' said Mally with a smile and sat down next to me on the sofa.

'And how's school?' said Mum.

'Fine, thanks,' said Mally.

Mum seemed at a loss.

'Something smells good,' said Mally after a moment.

'Yes, it's roast beef. Oh God! You do eat beef, don't you?'

'Yes, don't worry. It's pork we don't eat,' said Mally.

'Oh, that's right, yes. How silly of me.'

Herbie rolled his eyes and turned back to his Xbox. This was a lot more awkward than I'd expected; but I'd never had a boyfriend round for lunch, so I didn't know what I was expecting really. I never used to think I wanted my boyfriend and my mother to get along, but now that I actually *had* a boyfriend I realised how important it was. The only one who seemed relaxed was Socks, lying on his back on a turret of cushions. I wished I was a dog.

After about a million years Mum said lunch should be ready by now and we all went through to the kitchen. She brought out a great hunk of roast beef from the oven, surrounded by a landscape of vegetables.

'Well, tuck in, all of you.'

Mum poured herself a glass of wine and for a while the only sounds in the kitchen were knives and forks scraping against plates. This wasn't going well.

'So Lucy tells me some of your family still live in Bangladesh,' she said.

'Cousins, yeah.'

'I hear they've been devastated by floods and so on.'

'Yeah, it hasn't been good.'

'How terrible. It must be so difficult for them.'

'*Mum.*' I was blushing, I didn't know who for. Mum was basically being really uncool, in the way mums are. But Mally didn't seem to mind.

'It is difficult, yes. But I don't know that, you know, it's exactly like you imagine. I mean, not everyone's miserable, eating, like, dirt or whatever. A couple of years ago Bangladesh came top in the World Happiness Survey.'

'Is there such a thing?' asked Mum.

'It was done by the London School of Economics,' said Mally.

'Where did Britain come?'

'Thirty-second,' said Mally.

'But that doesn't make any sense,' I said. 'Why would they be happy when they've got nothing and we've got everything?'

'I know, it's weird. But I think that's exactly the point. Over here we're always wanting more when we don't actually *need* anything. Over there, if people have what they need, they don't particularly *want* anything else.'

'But still, their situation is pretty crappy,' I said.

'Yeah, materially it is. But there's a lot more acceptance of their situation than there would be over here. The most important thing to everyone is that their family is happy. They don't think they should go out and be a celebrity or whatever.'

'Well, maybe you should spend less time reading those celebrity mags of yours, Lucy, and more time thinking about the happiness of your family,' said Mum.

'Yeah. You can stop hogging the bathroom for a start,' said Herbie.

'*Herbie.* As if.'

'What were you doing this morning? You were in there for hours,' he said.

'*Herbie,* thanks a lot. I wasn't long at all.' Great, I really needed my bathroom habits to be discussed in front of Mally.

But Mally just smiled at me. 'At school in Bangladesh every child learns the fable of the king who is hugely rich but still unhappy. A wise man tells the king that he will only recover if he wears a happy man's shirt. Ministers search everywhere, all the big mansions, all the successful men. But they can't find one. At last they come across a man working in the woods; he has no house, no money. But he says he is happy.'

'So the king is cured, right?' said Herbie.

'No, because the man has no shirt,' said Mally.

We looked at him blankly.

'I think it means that only the poor, who can't afford to wear a shirt, are happy,' said Mally.

'What a lovely story,' I said, secretly thinking that having no shirts would seriously suck. 'Does that mean shirts are bad?'

'I don't think it's meant to be taken literally,' said Mally.

'Phew!' I said.

'Oh, I get it.' Mally grinned at me. 'I love your T-shirts. I love all your clothes. They're very cool.'

After lunch Mally and I went upstairs and lay on the bed in my room. I felt a little self-conscious to be honest. My room was looking pretty bare. I'd taken down the cheesy posters, but I hadn't got round to replacing them with anything else. And I felt full and fat.

Mally was lying next to me, propped up on one elbow. I sucked my tummy in.

'Mally, you don't think I'm shallow, do you?' I asked. I was fishing for compliments but I needed reassurance.

'Shallow?' Mally burst out laughing. 'You are the least shallow person I've ever met. You're thoughtful and kind and you care about things. Why can't you care about what you look like too? I know I do.'

'I knew it! I knew that look had some planning behind it. All those just-tight-enough black T-shirts, and jeans that fit you perfectly. You must have gone through about fifty pairs to find them.' I punched him playfully on the shoulder.

'Yeah yeah,' said Mally, rolling me on to my back.

'What else d'you like about me?' I said. Now I was *badly* fishing for compliments, but . . . I'd never had a boy be so amazing to me before. What's a girl supposed to do?

'I like the fact that when I'm with you I feel free,' said Mally. Then he paused. 'Free from all . . . the rest of my life. I never thought I'd fall so hard for anyone right now. It just wasn't part of my game plan. I thought I'd have my head buried in a book for the last year of school. But then *you* came along and I realised what I'd been missing. I don't have to be *only* serious and hard-working, I can have a laugh too, just goof off. It's not a question of absolutes.'

'Huh?'

'I mean, I can do both. You're the best, most funniest

person I know. And after I've been with you I feel refreshed, so I can work even harder. It's a win-win situation!' Mally kissed me playfully.

'Great,' I said with a pout. 'I'm just the good-time girl. And FYI, "most funniest" won't win you any gold stars in your father's book.'

'Most funny. Funniest. Hell, I'll say what I want,' said Mally, burying his face into my neck until I was screeching.

'OK, OK, say what you want – I give in!'

'Do you? Do you give in?' said Mally, still growling.

'Yesss. Yes I do.'

Then we kissed and everything went dark in my head, except for a few bright points of light that spun around and around. When I opened my eyes again I found Mally already looking at me.

'You know the amazing thing though?' he said.

'What?' I said, blinking exaggeratedly, like a silent film star.

'If I tell you, you'll think I'm weird.'

'No, I won't! I mean, I think you're weird already, so it won't make much of a difference. Tell me.'

Mally pulled me close to him and sighed. 'It's a bit of a long story. But I've never told anyone – any girl – about it before.'

'Tell me,' I said again, torn between glowing with pride and being upset that we weren't going to kiss any more.

'It's about going back to Bangladesh when I was ten. My "identity update" I call it.'

'Go on,' I said, snuggling closer. That would have to do instead of lip action.

'I hated it at first. Everyone was so poor. They were filthy, nobody had any shoes on. This was where my parents came from, the place I had always been told was home, but it felt so . . . it felt so foreign.'

'I can imagine,' I said, even though I couldn't really.

'It was hot out there and I mean *really* hot. No electricity, no fans or air-con, nothing. One morning I went to the mosque next to the house because I'd noticed how cool the floor was. It was made of marble, I think. I lay on the floor all day. I felt so peaceful. Everything just seemed to drop away. Every day after that I went into the mosque first thing in the morning, before anyone, and lay there for hours. Tareque was on at me; he said I was showing off by pretending to be a devout Muslim, but that wasn't it.'

'It wasn't?' I said.

I must have looked a bit worried because Mally looked at me and said, 'I knew you were going to think I'm weird, a fanatic or something.'

'No no! Of course I don't,' I said. But if I'm totally honest, I did feel a bit weird. Mosques and Muslims were usually something I saw in the paper and usually to do with something bad. 'Sooo, you're a Muslim then?' I asked.

'Yeah, I'm a Muslim. Don't look at me like that! I'm not going to put you in a veil or anything. It's me, Mally!' He kissed me on the nose. 'But that's exactly my point. I felt different over there, but when I came back to England I realised I was different from everybody here too.'

He paused for a minute.

'And that's what's so amazing. When I'm with you I forget about all that stuff. It doesn't matter if I'm Bangladeshi, or British, or brainy, or stupid. Whether my favourite dinner is reshmi kebab or fish and chips. It doesn't matter. When I'm around you I just feel like I'm . . . me. Does that make any sense?'

My anxiety dropped away. 'Totally! I feel exactly the same. I mean, I'm just plain old English with some Scottish thrown in, but I feel like I can be *me* around you. Even though we haven't *properly* known each other that long. I feel like I've known you all my life.'

Mally kissed me again. Then he drew back and stared at me. He looked very serious all of a sudden. My heart started to beat very loudly.

Love Divided

'I love you,' he said.

It was exactly what I had been feeling.

'I love you too. I love you!'

I reached up and kissed him. I wanted to drown in him.

'You know that happy man in your story? I'd be happy like him, if I had no shirt, no house or anything. As long as I had you.'

Chapter 5

♥

When summer term started, Mally and I couldn't see each other all day, every day, as we had in the holidays. But we tried to squeeze in as much time together as we could. I wanted to be with him all the time. I knew how a drug addict felt. I went into Mally-withdrawal during lessons (there should be posters up at school: *Parents, beware, keep your children from the dangerous new drug* Mally!) and found it really hard to concentrate. So by lunchtime I was desperate for a fix. The only problem was that Rachel came to meet me too and I had to tell her that I couldn't hang out with the usual gang at lunch because I was spending it with Mally. But I was sure Rachel understood – I was in love. If I'm completely honest, any time spent apart from Mally right then was time wasted, and that included my friends.

Exams were very definitely starting to loom on the horizon and Mally sometimes put in a couple of hours of homework in the library in the evening. I had to work too, although I wasn't under quite as much pressure as Mally. We sat beside each other as the light outside faded to darkness. Sometimes I used to rest my head on my arm and let myself daydream: Mally and I grown up and married, both working in jobs we loved and coming home to sit side by side, not talking, just happy to be together, just like we were now. What would our kids look like? If they were half as cute as Mally . . . then I'd glance sideways at him and blush a little. We hadn't talked about any of this stuff; even if I did write *Lucy Khan* in curly writing down the side of my notepad, I made sure he didn't see it. It was just a daydream . . . wasn't it?

It was shocking to discover that, even when I was so happy, things could still go wrong. The day started off badly. First Socks knocked an entire glass of orange juice over my new T-shirts that I'd made for global warming *and* my chemistry homework. Then Mr Skelton didn't believe me, and he gave me *more* homework, as well as making me redo the last lot.

When I went to meet Mally at lunchtime he'd had a crappy morning too. He had got a B in an economics essay – hard to believe but that's what made up a crappy morning for him. We were both pissed off, sitting on a bench outside the school gates with Ehsan – who loved it when, occasionally, Mally hung out with him for lunch – munching dolefully on our sandwiches. We badly needed cheering up.

Here's how the fateful conversation went:

Me: Let's go to Barbados!

Mally: Or Skegness!

Me: Skegness? London would be better than Skegness.

Mally: London *would* be better. Why don't we go to London?

We both looked at each other. We knew we could go to London quite easily: it was only half an hour away by train. We'd both been there loads of times before and it meant we could spend the whole afternoon together. Only we had lessons. Mally had economics. I had English.

Me: London could be part of our education. Dickens lived there. It's the economic centre of the world.

Mally: It'd be wrong *not* to go!

Ehsan looked at us both like we were mad. But he was only ten, what would he know? So we walked him back to his school and then went straight to the train station.

So that's how we came to be standing outside Buckingham Palace at three-thirty p.m. on a Wednesday, taking pictures of each other trying to stroke the guardsman's hat. We had decided to be tourists for the day; we figured that just because we had both been to London before didn't mean we couldn't be tourists. I mean, neither of us actually *lived* there.

So we did what tourists do. We walked across St James's Park holding hands and sharing an ice-cream even though it was spitting with rain. In the middle of the park Mally turned around and gave me absolutely the longest kiss *ever* and told me he loved me. I thought my heart would burst out of my chest with happiness.

By the time we got to the Houses of Parliament we were starving, and there were no cafés anywhere. We eventually found a picture of a man wearing a sign that said *CAFÉ*, only it seemed to point straight into the ground. Then we saw an ancient heavy door beneath the street. We looked at each other and shrugged; after all, we *were* on an adventure. Inside there were no windows and the whole place smelled of damp and we were just beginning to get freaked out, but we turned a corner and suddenly there was the *sweetest* old lady standing behind a huge tea-urn. Another equally old lady came to take our order; by now we didn't feel like tourists at all, but People of the Overground who had stumbled in on an ancient subterranean world. The best thing of all though was the dessert, which was huge and called a Double Chocolate Fudge Sundae Surprise, with ice-cream and cream and chocolate sauce and a flake all crammed into a tall glass. It came with two long spoons, and Mally and I kept clashing spoons trying to get to the most chocolatey bits.

I'll remember this moment for the rest of my life, I thought.

Usually I just carry on with life and only realise I've been happy when I look back. But this time I knew it then and there, and I wanted to make time stand still so I could feel this way for ever.

'I love you,' I told him.

'I love you too.'

We didn't seem to be able to stop saying it.

When Mally and I came blinking out into the sunlight we decided that the only way we'd really see all the sights was to be among our own people again – the Tourist People. So we caught an open-topped double-decker bus. It'd be educational, I said, though actually I hadn't given skipping my English class a second thought. And it *was* educational – in a way. The guide explained the history of the landmarks we were passing, how the original London Bridge had been sold to an American and was now in Arizona. Sometimes he threw in some cheesy jokes –

'You won't see any animals at Piccadilly Circus,' type stuff and everyone groaned.

It had started to rain but it was still hot and muggy. It felt as if we were floating above London in a ship. Mally looked so beautiful. The rain had spiked his hair and stuck to his eyelashes. It ran in miniature rivulets down his skin and made his T-shirt cling to his chest. I stared at him; he almost looked too real, as if he was in a movie.

'What?' he said.

'Nothing,' I said. 'Just that you're beautiful.'

'YOU are beautiful,' Mally said. He reached for his camera. 'Don't close your eyes like you usually do! Seriously. The rain really brings out who you are. Like it's washed you and made you shine.'

I smiled. Then he threw his arm around my neck and held the camera out in front of us.

'Perfect!'

It wasn't too bad, I suppose: my head was tilted up and my hair was in wisps around my face. I was half smiling, half wistful. Mally's beautiful almond-shaped eyes shone and he was looking straight into the camera.

He pulled the ring from the Coke can he'd been drinking from and slipped it on to my finger. It could have been the cheesiest thing, but in that moment it was so romantic. 'I want to be with you till I'm eighty,' he said.

'I want to be with you till I'm eighty-five,' I replied.

'Oh yeah? Well you've outdone me again.'

Then we kissed, and the whole of London passed by before we looked up again.

I was still wearing the Coke can ring Mally had given me on the bus, only my hands were thrust into my pockets and it was pressing painfully into my skin, when Mr Khan began to shout.

It had been a bit of a shock to see him in my kitchen when we got home. Mr Khan wanted to know where we'd been, though he already knew we'd been to London – Ehsan had told him. But Mr Khan wanted to know *precisely* where we'd been, and he made us tell him, though with each place we said he grew increasingly angry. My mum was cross too, though not as furious as Mr Khan.

'It is all very well going to *London,*' he leaned on the word with disgust. 'But what about your lessons, eh?'

'*Sorry*, Dad, it was only one lesson and it was revision. I can catch it up from Raj.'

'But it is not the same as being there, is it? *Is it?*' said Mr Khan.

'Not exactly,' said Mally, shifting from foot to foot.

'I really don't see how you could have been so

irresponsible to have missed lessons. Exams aren't far away. What could you have been thinking?'

Herbie had come into the kitchen. He'd obviously heard all the noise. 'What's wrong, Mum?'

'Nothing, sweetie,' said Mum, reaching out for him and pulling him in front of her. 'We're just having a discussion.'

'The trip was my idea, Mr Khan. I'm very, very sorry,' I said, trying to hold back my tears.

'No, it wasn't. It was my idea,' said Mally. 'Dad, please, can we just go?'

'IN A MINUTE, MALADHAR. Let me finish, please.'

Herbie looked really upset. He put his glasses back on and scrunched up his face, the way he does when he doesn't want to let anything bad in. But Mr Khan didn't notice. He spoke more quietly, but if anything it was more scary than before.

'Forgive me, Mrs Brooks, if I speak out of turn. But whilst you may be willing to let your daughter run around London on a school day, *I* am not willing to allow my son the same privilege. He has most important exams coming up, and all the family is most keen he should join his brother at university. If he should forfeit his place because of your daughter, it would be most . . .' Mr Khan seemed to search around for the right word, '. . . *unsuitable.*'

'But I'm not trying to make Mally forfeit his place!' I burst out. 'I want him to do well.'

'Well, you are certainly not showing it,' said Mr Khan, giving me a horrible look.

'Let me talk now, Mr Khan,' said my mum. 'I did not know that the two of them were in London this afternoon and I resent the implication that I am not strict enough with my daughter. You know nothing about me, or how I choose to bring my children up, and you are in *my* house. I think it's best if you and Mally leave now.'

Mally and I could only look at each other silently. Then I went up to my room and burst into tears.

Mum grounded me for two weeks. She was pretty angry with me. I understood why, so I didn't make too much fuss about being grounded. But it had all been worth it, in my opinion. I had had one of the best days of my life. Obviously Mally's dad was even more angry than my mum. A lot more angry. He grounded Mally for *three* weeks and during that time he hired a tutor to give him extra lessons *after* school too. Apparently he thought Mally wasn't taking his A-levels seriously enough.

I don't know where he got that idea. We might have

bunked off for one poxy afternoon, but if he'd known Mally like I knew him, he never would have thought he wasn't serious. He was incredibly dedicated and hard-working; he just happened to love me too.

Mally apologised a lot for his father. He said that his dad only wanted the best for him, but that he didn't know how to rein in his temper.

'But is everything OK now? I mean, your dad doesn't still hate me, does he?'

Mally laughed awkwardly. 'Oh no, it's fine. Honestly. He's still a bit angry with me though, and he's probably right. I can't afford to waste an afternoon at this point in my life.'

A little sliver of ice pushed its way into my heart. 'Is that what you thought our trip was, a wasted afternoon?'

'No, Luce, I didn't mean that! We had a great time. I just meant, we probably shouldn't have gone, at least, not now. I've never done anything like that before.'

'But I thought that's what you loved about me, the fact that you didn't have to be your old self all the time!'

'I do, Lucy, I do.' Mally put an arm around my waist. 'I'm just saying we probably shouldn't have gone, that's all.'

'Well, I'm *glad* we went,' I said, with a quivering lip. 'I had an *amazing* time. I would have given up my last day on earth to go to London with you. Obviously it's not the same for you.'

A thought flashed into my mind: *I miss my best friend.* I needed to speak to Rachel about this.

Mally spun me to face him. 'Lucy, don't be like that. I love you. I just need to work right now. It's different for you. You only have GCSEs and you . . .'

'And I what?'

'Nothing.

'And I don't care as much anyway?' I said, my voice trembling with anger.

'I wasn't going to say that exactly. Just that you probably don't want to go to Cambridge.'

'How do you know where I want to go? I'm just as ambitious as you are! I'm just not going to be a lawyer, or a doctor, that's all!'

'It's OK. Look, I'm sorry. I didn't mean it. I know you're going to be amazing. You are amazing!' Mally stroked my hair as if I was a child. 'I had a fantastic time in London. I'll remember it for ever. I love you. Let's just forget this conversation, OK?'

But I couldn't forget it. And we didn't say much else as we walked to the school gates and went our separate ways.

Chapter 6

♥

Exams were steaming towards Mally and me like a runaway train. Most of our lessons were revision, but then there were revision essays, and some of the books I had been supposed to read the first time round, I hadn't, so I had new stuff as well. Mally didn't have that problem, of course, but there was massive pressure on him because he was trying to get into Cambridge and he had to get three A's. And he had a load of extra-curricular activities too, to put on his CV; mainly projects he was doing on global warming.

I'd thought about it and I had to admit Mally might have been right – an afternoon off *did* have more consequences for him than it did for me right now. I tried not to worry about how we would keep our relationship going when Mally was away at university – Cambridge wasn't that far and they had super-long holidays. Love would find a way, I thought.

The weekends were our precious time together – our time to do whatever we wanted. Which was usually nothing, just lazing about in my room together, kissing and listening to music. It was just nice to relax.

On this particular weekend though I had planned to surprise Mally with something special. I'd read in the local paper that they were showing a Bollywood film in a cinema nearby. It was quite difficult to get tickets – it was in an arthouse cinema that never seemed to answer the phone and it didn't have a proper website to buy them on either, so I had to go all the way over on the bus and buy them from the box office. The film starred a new Bengali girl who was meant to be fantastic; she was a big heroine in Bangladesh. Mally always complained that there weren't enough Bengali stars in England so I figured he'd be really pleased to see her. I was so excited about my surprise I nearly blurted it out a thousand times, but I made myself wait until just a few days before the weekend so that the surprise would be even greater. I just couldn't wait to see the look on his face – I knew he'd be totally over the moon.

'I have got an amazing Saturday night lined up for you, Maladhar Khan,' I said in my best game-show voice. 'First we travel by five star coach – well, it's the bus really – over to Brinton. A quick change, and then it's off to —'

'Lucy, I'm really sorry, I can't make Saturday.'

My heart plummeted and I nearly dropped the phone.

'Oh . . . but . . . it's all planned. I mean, I thought you'd be thrilled. I bought tickets to the new Bollywood film, especially . . .

'I'm really sorry, Looooceee,' he said, in the teasing way he usually used to get round me. 'I'd love to come, you know I would, only I can't. One of my cousins is getting married.'

'Oh, right. Where?'

'At Aunt Shefali's house in London.'

'What – is her daughter getting married? She didn't mention it!'

'No, it's her sister's – my other aunt's – daughter. They live in a tiny flat, so Aunt Shefali is having the wedding at her house. Well, in the garden, really.'

'Right.' My first thought was: *Why didn't you tell me about this earlier?* And right on the heels of that: *Why didn't you invite me?* Even though I didn't know the bride, I knew Aunt Shefali and Uncle Rafiq. And I thought Mally would want me there. But maybe the wedding was really small. 'How many people are going?'

'Oh, not many. About two hundred, I think.'

'Two hundred! Wow! That's many in my book. It's . . .' I paused.

'It's annoying, I know. I'm really sorry,' said Mally.

'No, I mean, it's just quite weird you didn't mention

this to me before. I've gone to all this trouble with the tickets, and I wouldn't have bothered if I'd known you were busy.'

'Yeah, I know, it slipped my mind – stupid of me . . .' Mally sounded awkward.

I bet lots of people were bringing their girlfriends. If it had been the other way round I would have been desperate to have Mally there.

Mally seemed to know what I was thinking. 'I didn't ask you to come . . . I mean . . . I didn't think you'd like it. You'd know hardly anyone and it would be weird for you. It's not like an English wedding.'

It sounded like just the kind of thing I'd love.

'You'd probably get bored. It goes on the whole weekend and —'

'I love weddings. I've heard so much about Bengali weddings. They sound amazing,' I said, thinking I was making it really obvious.

'Mmm, I don't. All that eating and sitting around.'

'Yeah. That's what's great about them.'

'Mmm,' said Mally again. He sounded even more awkward now. 'Perhaps we could go another evening? To the cinema. Another weekend I'm totally at your disposal.'

'I've already bought the tickets for *this* weekend.'

'Of course. Look I'm really sorry, Lucy. I promise you, the weekend after this we'll do something really special, OK?'

After I'd put the phone down I almost burst into tears. I didn't believe him when he said I would find it boring. I'd told him I loved weddings. It was really weird of him to have forgotten to tell me. And I'd made such an effort to treat him to something really special. Now the tickets would go to waste.

Usually Mally and I talked about everything. This was just the kind of thing I'd normally go to him with for advice. Only this time, it was *about* him.

Maybe I could persuade Rachel to come instead, but I didn't know if she even liked Bollywood films. And I hadn't seen her in a while; I just hoped she wasn't busy too.

'A *Bollywood* film?' said Rachel. 'Why aren't you taking Mally?'

'It's a long story. Do you fancy it?'

'I don't know.'

'Please come, Rach. Please please please!'

'I haven't seen you in ages,' she said, accusingly.

'I know and I'm really sorry. I'll buy you dinner!'

So, by blatantly bribing my best friend, I got her to come. I realised that over the last few weeks I'd missed phoning Rachel at any time of the day or night. Even though I was totally over the moon and besotted with Mally, at least some of the pleasure of that feeling was sharing it with my best friend.

Before the movie we had a cup of tea in the cinema café. Rachel was a bit quiet at first, not her usual noisy self. So I just came right out and said it.

'Look, Rach, I'm really sorry we haven't been hanging out so much. I've missed you.'

'It's OK,' she said, in a way that obviously meant it *wasn't*.

'Really?' I said. 'Are you sure?'

'Umm. It's just, I feel a bit second best. I mean, you only asked me tonight because Mally couldn't come. Whenever he's around you don't want to know.'

'You're right. You're completely right,' I said, blushing with shame. 'It's just that, I don't know, being in love has taken me over. It's like, I don't have room for anything else. Or I didn't.'

'But I've been out with loads of boys. Have I ever not included you?'

'Weeeell,' I thought about it. 'There was that time we were meant to be going to the cinema. With Dan, wasn't it? You kept me waiting forty minutes . . .'

'I know, I know, and we missed the film. That was

Dan's fault. His car broke down. But I showed up.'

'And then there was that time we were meant to be going out for my birthday, only you brought Cato along.'

'But Cato was really sweet!'

'He was sweet. But it was meant to be just us. I felt like a gooseberry; he kept trying to snog you on the way to the toilet. And then there was Andrew; we were meant to be going shopping that time —'

Rachel burst out laughing. 'OK, OK, point taken.'

'Look, I've realised that friends are really important too, and you're the most important friend I've got. And I promise to call you from now on, even when Mally *is* around.'

Rachel gave me a big grin and flicked her hair back over her shoulders. 'OK. You're forgiven. Anyway, I have something to confess too.'

I looked at her quizzically.

'I've been avoiding you a bit too.'

'Oh God, Rach! What, because you were so pissed off?'

'No, silly! I have to admit, well, I was a little bit jealous.'

I was amazed. 'Jealous? Of me? But you always have loads of boyfriends!'

'That's just it. I always have loads of boyfriends but they're all crappy. You have lucked out on the very first one.'

'Second one – Quintin Tiptree, remember!'

'Second one then. But I've had about a million and I've never felt serious about any of them. I mean, I'm not serious about Sam either.'

'*Sam?*'

'Haven't I told you? My new boyfriend, in the year above.'

'Oh, *that* Sam!' I said, even though I had no idea who he was; our school was pretty big. 'But that's great!'

'It's not serious though. It just happened the other day.'

'Oh . . . but still . . . it's exciting.'

'Yeah. I don't feel the same as you feel about Mally, but I like him. It's cool.'

'I don't know that . . . I mean, you're only meant to fall in love once or twice in your whole life, right? I might have used mine up on the very first go. You've got ages.'

'Yeah . . . So what's it like, being in luuurve?' said Rachel. 'I mean, we've watched so many movies about being in love – is it like that?' It was really strange *her* asking *me* about this stuff. Usually she was dispensing advice. I could see it was strange for Rachel too. She was fiddling with her hair and looking at me sideways.

'It is the same as in movies, yeah. When I think of Mally my heart feels as if it's soaring over the clouds. Sometimes if I'm just doing something boring like walking down the street I've got this great big orchestra playing in my head.'

'Or maybe you've got your iPod on!'

We laughed.

'I think of him at least once a minute when I'm not with him – everything seems to lead back to him and then it's as if my heart gets a tiny electric shock. I don't know how I went through sixteen years without him.'

'Wow,' said Rachel.

'But then, you know, it doesn't mean everything is perfect. I was really upset he didn't invite me to the wedding this weekend.'

'Maybe he thought you'd be bored.'

'That's what he said. I wouldn't have been though.'

'But by then it was probably too late to invite you along,' said Rachel.

'Maybe. All I know is, *I* wouldn't want to go anywhere without Mally by my side.'

'That's a good thing though, right?'

'Yeah. I just hope there's not something weird going on,' I said.

'No! Like what?'

'I dunno. Probably nothing. I'm just a bit worried that Mally's family is totally different from mine. He has so many more family commitments.'

'But you and Mally are soulmates, right? That's all that matters.'

'Yeah, I guess.'

'I know Mally should have been here with you today, and he isn't,' said Rachel. 'But I'm glad you asked me to come instead.'

'You don't mind missing out on a Saturday with Sam?' I said.

'Sam? No, it's cool. And you're not missing Mally too much?'

'Not now that we're solid again,' I said, kissing her on the cheek.

Chapter 7

♥

With just a few weeks to go until exams I sat down and made a timetable. Every day would follow a strict routine. Get up at seven a.m. and do an hour's work before breakfast. From nine a.m. to one p.m. I was either in lessons or revising in the library. Lunchtime – one hour off. Two p.m. till four p.m. – in lessons or revising in the library. Break until five p.m. Then working at home till six p.m. when I would collapse in front of the TV.

Most lunchtimes I'd text Mally, or he'd text me, and we'd meet in our café. Believe it or not, I'd grown quite fond of cappuccinos. They helped my concentration. Then I'd test Mally on some fiendishly difficult maths or economics question that *obviously* I wouldn't know the answer to, and I'd have to skim through the whole of his files to find it, which took hours. I didn't think I was being very helpful, but Mally said just having me around was helpful enough.

Some lunchtimes I'd meet him and he'd have black

circles under his eyes. He said he was fine; he wouldn't say what time he'd stayed up till the night before, but I had a feeling it was late. On those days I worried for him – I mean there is such a thing as working *too* hard. Mally drank a lot of coffee and sometimes his hands shook – too much caffeine, he said. But when I said he was working too hard, he smiled and shook his head. There was no such thing as too hard, he said. He really wanted to do something with his life; what was so wrong with that? Nothing, I said, nothing at all. Then I'd put my hands over his and lean into him and let his head rest on my shoulder. He smelled so good, of shampoo and pencils and an indefinable Malliness that I wanted to bottle up and keep next to my bed for ever, and I'd feel all his stress drop away and I'd know he still needed me.

This relationship was the REAL THING. Mally had turned out to be so much more than any Dream Guy I could have thought up. He wasn't like those boys (cringe) that I used to have on my bedroom wall, all chisel-jawed and ripped pecs. He didn't have a motorbike, or even a car; he didn't have a record deal. We hadn't met in a trendy, crowded bar – far from it! He could be quiet, even moody. Occasionally he had spots. But I loved him. I just wished it could be pure and uncomplicated, like it had been in the beginning. I wished Mally didn't put himself under so much pressure. I wished he could just be mine, away from all his other commitments. It was selfish of me, I know, but a tiny part of me wished he had a small family, just like mine, that made no demands on him. But he didn't, and there was nothing I could do about it.

When Mally and I needed a break we went to the football field. My bum was so numb from all that sitting, and my legs were crooked like an old lady's, and I'd just want to run and shout to release some of the pressure. Then Mally would grab my hand and we'd sprint about, laughing hysterically.

So you see, even though there were exams and everything was crazy all around us, we were still happy.

One afternoon I really really didn't feel like going to the library. I know it meant breaking my routine but I was sick to death of the sight of it. So I asked Mally if we could go to his house to revise – we could do just the same amount of work there *and* we could have a cup of tea at the same time.

'Oh yeah. Sure,' he said.

'Great!'

'Only, hang on a minute. I think my dad's home and there might be, you know, some cousins coming later. I actually think it might be a bit mad over there to work.'

'Oh, OK. But shouldn't I see your dad again? I don't think I made a very good impression last time.'

'You did! I mean, it's fine. Though you two should meet again, definitely. Only maybe not today. He's got a lot on.'

In the end we went to the library. Again. We spent so much time there we should have our own chairs with little plaques on them.

When I got home I realised I hadn't been to Mally's house since I went over for lunch that time. I was on the computer, pretending to work, but actually I had done so much revision that day I just wanted to chill out. I noticed Rachel was on MSN.

Hey yooooooo. How goes it?

Looo C. Wot you doing MSNing me u shld be WORKING?

I KNOW I've had it for today. Can I ask you a q???

Go ahead . . .

I've never been to Mally's house to revise. Izit weird?

It's a bit weird.
Actually not that weird.
I've hardly been to ne of my X's houses.

O ok.
But I asked if we could go round today and Mally
said NO.
Relatives were ova.

Then DATS why you couldn't go you FREAK.
Wots problemo?

Don't think his dad likes me.
After THAT row.
Wot u think??????

Then I just stared at the cursor blinking on and off. I
stared at it until my eyes burned, thinking about Mally's
dad.

Where r u? I typed finally.

Hang on sweeeeets Ian jus texted.

Ian?????

Ian my new boyfriend.

Wottt????? I didn't even know Sam was out the window, let alone Ian in.
Wot bout Sam?? I typed.

It's ova.
Wosn't going newhere.
I'm seeing a new boy now.
Ian.
South End Ian.

Wow. This was pretty quick, even for Rachel. I had heard of the South End Crew. They hung about in tracksuits (not a look Rachel usually liked), talking like black guys, even though they were all white. I was a bit surprised . . . maybe she was on the rebound. Then again, nothing ought to surprise me about Rachel.

Gr8, I typed.
Is it cooool??

Yeahh.
It's fine. He's fit.

Love Divided

When did it happen?

*2day!!!!! He kissed me in bus shelter waiting 4 da no.
52 bus. Row Man Tic ehhhhh???*

Wowjeeeee. Did u heart go PITAPAT??

Kindaaa. He's got big arms.

Awwwww.

But you should go ova 2 Mally's.
Surprise him.
*Dress nice and make nicey wiv Mr Khan then you
don't hav 2 worry that u've neva seen his house NE
MORE.*

You think??????

TOTALLY.
Mally's dropped over unannounced 2 u rite?

Mmmhmm.

Then wot's the prob?

DO IT.

Maybe I WILL!!!!!
Can't hurt right?

You know it girl!

Thanks Rach.
U r wicked on a stick.

O I know! Betta sign off now. Hugs n kisses xxxx

I decided to take Rachel's advice. At lunchtime the next day I figured I'd surprise Mally by bringing a takeaway latte to his doorstep – grande, two shots, full fat, just how he liked it. Mr Khan was bound to be at the restaurant. Only, when I reached his house, it was Mr Khan who answered the door. He looked surprised to see me.

'Lucy, isn't it?' he said, and he just stood there with the door half open.

His hair was swept back, and he was immaculately turned out in a suit and a very white shirt and shoes that shone as brightly as a dog's nose. In all the times I had seen him, Mr Khan had struck me as a great big man, but actually he wasn't. He just seemed big.

'Hello, Mr Khan, yeah, it's Lucy.'

'And you have come . . . to see Mally, I presume? Or is it another matter I can help you with?'

'Oh no. Mally. Thanks! I brought him some coffee. To help his concentration, you know, for revising and stuff.'

'I see. Good. Well, you'd better come in.'

Mr Khan showed me into the lounge. I hadn't been in this room on my last visit. It was much neater than the sitting room in my house. In fact it looked as if nobody ever went in there. There was a large beige sofa with cushions arranged on their points, a complicated geometrical rug that obviously wasn't meant for walking on and a big framed picture with Arabic writing on the wall. I sat down gingerly on the tip of the sofa: it would be a nightmare to spill coffee over it. Mr Khan smiled a wide smile – too wide actually; it looked as if his face might break open with the effort of it. Then he left and I heard his footsteps going upstairs. I could hear someone – Mally's mother, I supposed – clanking around in the kitchen, but she didn't come through. Ehsan would be at school. Sitting there I wasn't so sure I had made the right decision coming here after all.

I heard some muffled voices coming through the wall. 'Why mmmphff mmmphff restaurant, Dad? I mean you didn't really mmffshhff home in the first place.'

'I don't want to have any person in my kitchen cupboards! Easier to come home than to explain which pot. Exercise will do me good.' Mr Khan's voice came through loud and clear. 'You had better go and see your friend.'

Then Mally came through the door, looking flustered. 'Hi, Lucy. What are you doing here?'

'I . . . I . . . um . . . came to bring you coffee? Sorry I didn't text you first; I thought, I thought it'd be OK to come over and revise. Are your relatives still here?'

Just then Mr Khan appeared and gave me another stiff smile and motioned for me to sit back down. I wished I hadn't bought the stupid coffee now. I felt too awkward to hand it to Mally but it was even worse trying not to spill it.

'Lucy. How is your revising going?'

'Oh, OK thank you, Mr Khan. Mally's been really useful actually. We go to the coffee house and —'

'Lucy has GCSEs,' Mally cut in quickly. 'She's doing ten subjects.'

'Which coffee house?' asked Mr Khan.

'Umm, Costa? The leather armchairs, they're, umm comfy.' I tried to smile at Mally — we had a private joke about those armchairs. But he didn't smile back.

'And can you concentrate where people are drinking coffee?' said Mr Khan.

'Oh yes, we test each other,' I said.

Mr Khan took a deep breath in before he spoke. 'Test each other. And do you know anything about the subjects upon which Maladhar is sitting his exams?'

'Not too much, but . . .' I looked at Mally.

'It's fine, Dad. We work,' said Mally. 'I go to the library mainly.'

I began to have the feeling Mally hadn't told his dad how much we hung out. But I wished he could have had a CCTV strapped to our foreheads, then he could see we did nothing *but* work. And snog, but that was getting less.

'And what is your favourite subject, Lucy?' asked Mr Khan.

'Umm. Fashion, I think. Or English.'

'Fashion. I see,' said Mr Khan. 'What exactly do you study in fashion?'

'Oh, there's lots of things. History of fashion . . . how to cut a pattern, that kind of thing.'

'How to cut a pattern,' Mr Khan repeated. 'And is that useful?'

Something in the way he said, 'Is that useful?' made me cross. It was as if he was saying that I was use*less*. First he made out that Mally and I did no work when we actually *did*. Now he was saying my subjects were rubbish. I could feel myself starting to blush, but for once, instead of embarrassment, I felt anger. And then whoomphff, there it came, until I was glowing like a red lightbulb.

'Yes,' I said hotly. 'Clothes can be quite useful. You know, for wearing?'

Great, I'd really blown it now. First London, now an argument about the usefulness of clothes. Out of nowhere the story Mally had told us at dinner, about the man with no shirt, popped into my head. Nice one, Lucy, way to pick an argument.

Mr Khan didn't flinch but his eyes narrowed. 'I dare say,' he said in exactly the same tone. 'Fashion may be useful for some. What do you intend on doing with your fashion and English?'

Blimey – what did he want, a full career plan?

'She's quite good, Dad,' said Mally. 'She made some T-shirts at school. Everybody wore them.'

Thank goodness Mally had said something at last – I thought he'd lost the ability to speak.

'Actually I'm going to university to do textile design,' I said, in my poshest voice. I'd just made it up on the spot, but it sounded good, to me at least.

But obviously not to Mr Khan. 'I see,' he said, like he didn't see at all.

I needed to get out and I needed Mally to come with me to explain what the hell was going on.

'I should probably go,' I said. 'Got some revising to do.'

'Oh, OK. I'll see you out,' said Mally.

Why wasn't Mally coming with me? I needed to speak to him. But Mr Khan was right behind us the whole way through the hall to the front door. I didn't say anything. Mally didn't say anything, didn't even kiss me on the cheek as I left. And it was only when I got halfway down the street I noticed I still had his coffee in my hand.

Why the bloody hell had Mally let his father speak to me like that? Had he even *told* his father we hung out? Did Mr Khan even know we were *going out*?

Maybe I didn't know Mally very well, after all.

Mally's dad was so freakin' weird and he made Mally weird. The worst of it was that Mally had just sat there and said hardly anything the whole time his dad was being mean to me.

Work was out of the question and I didn't know what to do with myself. But before a minute had gone by Mally texted me: *Where are you?*

I didn't reply, I just shoved my phone into my pocket. I was fishing around for my keys; I still felt hot and red only now my face was wet with tears. Then I heard footsteps running up behind me.

Mally. He spun me round and tried to hug me. I pushed him off.

'Lucy! I am so sorry. About my dad. He doesn't mean it, he —'

'You haven't told, him have you? That we've been revising together. I bet you haven't even told him we're going out!'

'I have, I have! He knows we're going out. God, believe me, he *knows* you're my girlfriend.'

'But have you told him we've been revising together this whole time? *Have you*?'

Mally looked down. 'Most of the time, yeah.'

'*Most of the time*? What's so wrong with me? Why does your dad hate me?'

'He doesn't hate you – I mean, not you particularly.' Mally looked at his feet and fell silent.

I stood there. 'What d'you mean?'

'Look, Lucy, this is going to sound horrible. You know how I told you you're the first serious girlfriend I've ever had . . . ? You're also the first white girlfriend I've had . . .'

Right. What did that mean?

'The others were friends of my aunt and uncle. I don't think Dad is too keen on the idea that I'm going out with you.'

'But . . . why? Is it because we went to London that day?'

'Oh God, Lucy, this is really hard.' Mally hesitated. 'It's because . . . you're from England.'

'But so are you!' Then I understood. 'Oh, I get it. It's because I'm white.'

'Dad's got loads of white friends,' Mally hurried on. 'Nearly all his customers are white. He doesn't think white people are stupid, or, I don't know, uncultured or anything like that. He loves England. It's just that, when it comes to who his children date, it's different. He's made all these sacrifices so that we can get ahead, but part of the whole future he has imagined for us is that we all marry girls, you know, that he'd approve of.'

'Girls from Bangladesh.'

'Or a British-Bangladeshi, yeah.'

It was horrible – and weird – to hear that somebody didn't like me because of the colour of my skin. I felt so helpless. 'It's like the Dark Ages! And you? What do you think?'

'You know what I think! I love going out with you! But I can't change my father's mind. England is still a foreign country to him. He wants us all to be with someone from home.'

'Which home? What d'you mean – Bangladesh?'

'Yeah.'

'And what about your mum?'

'She likes you – they both like you.'

'But she agrees with your father.'

Mally was silent, which meant yes.

'But why did you let your dad speak to me like that if you love me? It was so humiliating!'

'I'm really sorry, Lucy. My dad was totally out of order. But it's his house. I have to respect that.'

'And that means not respecting me, obviously.'

'It's not like that! You don't understand.'

'So you keep saying.' As far as I was concerned, it *was* like that. 'If you really loved me you would have stuck up for me. Your dad is obviously a weirdo freak who likes to put down people and you just stand there watching.'

'Don't say that, sweetheart, you don't . . . you don't know him.'

'You see, you're *still* sticking up for him even when he hates me!' I started to cry.

'I'm not! I just can't explain.'

'Well, fine. You don't have to! I don't care either way. I'm obviously not worth explaining TO!' I tried to push the keys into the door, but I was crying so hard I couldn't see the keyhole.

'Look, my dad isn't a freak,' said Mally.

'Oh no, I forgot, he's a racist.'

Mally was silent.

I was crying so hard I don't know how I finally got the keys in the door, but I did. And I didn't even look at Mally before I slammed the door on him.

Chapter 8

♥

There was only one person I could turn to.
Rachel. And when I phoned her, sobbing
hysterically, she was there for me, right away. We
met in our old favourite spot, on the bench outside JD
Sports in the mini-mall; the inside-out bench we called it,
because it tried to pretend it was outside when actually it
was inside. I wasn't feeling much like being around
people, but I couldn't think where else to meet. I looked
a mess. My eyes were swollen from crying and my cheeks
were all blotchy and I was basically wearing a pair of
pyjamas, which I'd put on after the argument and hadn't
bothered taking off.

'Oh my God, Lucy, what's happened?' Rachel put her
arms around me and I broke out into fresh sobs.

'It's Mally. It's over.'

'No! Why?'

I was crying so hard people were starting to stare. I
drew my knees up and buried my face in them. Rachel
held me tight.

'What's happened? Tell me everything.'

It all came out in a rush: how Mally had admitted that his father didn't like me, how mean Mr Khan had been and how Mally hadn't stuck up for me.

'Why doesn't Mr Khan like you?' said Rachel.

'Because I'm not from Bangladesh. Friends are OK apparently, but girlfriends, no. They have to be from where Mally's from.'

'God. That's weird,' said Rachel.

'He hadn't told his dad that we revised together. His dad seemed totally shocked to see me.' I still had more tears left from somewhere and they spilled out on to my cheeks.

'But you know what? Mally must have told his dad you two were serious. Otherwise his dad wouldn't have been so freaky,' said Rachel.

'I suppose,' I sniffed. 'But he could have done a better job of sticking up for me.'

'Yes, you're right, sweetie. You're right.' Rachel still had her arm around me. 'But you can't blame Mally for having a difficult dad. I mean, it's not his fault.'

'But Mally was so *different* around him. The reason I loved him in the first place was that he wasn't afraid to stand up for anything.'

'And he still isn't. He came running after you, didn't

he, just a minute after you left? If his dad hates you that much he can't have liked that.'

'I guess. But then we had a row.' I gave another sob.

'You've said yourself how much respect Mally has for his family. And he did stand up for you a little bit, about the T-shirts?'

'He could have done a whole lot more. He was far more respectful to his dad than to me.'

'Well, I suppose we can't really understand,' said Rachel.

'That's what Mally kept saying. Anyway. It doesn't matter because we're over.'

'But you love him, don't you?'

'Yes,' I said simply. I loved Mally so much it hurt. 'I just wish he'd been honest with me and told me about his dad.'

'And what's he supposed to have said? Gee, Lucy, my dad doesn't really go for you, so I haven't told him that we're revising together? You would have gone mental.'

'I suppose . . . It does feel pretty horrible now that I know about it.' I squeezed Rachel's arm for support.

'Look sweetie, you're amazing. I know that and Mally knows that. It doesn't matter what his dad thinks.'

I had a feeling that it did. But Rachel did make sense. I couldn't really blame Mally for his dad. My own dad was no angel. I wrapped my arms round Rachel and gave her a massive hug. I felt better speaking to her. I'd been pretty self-obsessed recently – I hadn't even asked about her own love life.

'We're always talking about me lately,' I said. 'How's Ian?'

'Ian? He's OK, I suppose. He's pretty fit. But he's not that bright and he's not great company.'

'Why are you with him then?'

'I dunno. Because it's something to do?'

'How does it go – he's not Mr Right, he's Mr Right Now?'

'Totally.'

We smiled at each other.

'There's lots of time,' I said. 'It's not like we're sixty.'

'That's what you always say. Gotta kiss alotta frogs . . .'

'But maybe,' I said, 'you should set your standards a bit higher. You're so worth it. You're gorgeous, and you're smart and you're funny. What boy wouldn't go for you?'

'Yeah – what boy wouldn't?' Rachel puckered up her lips and crossed her eyes.

'You idiot! Seriously though, thanks, Rach. I don't know how I'd live without you, I really don't.'

'You'd be a gibbering wreck, that's how,' said Rachel, and she planted a big kiss in the middle of my forehead.

For a couple of days I didn't text Mally and he didn't text me. But one morning, when I checked my email, I saw Mally's name in my inbox. My heart started beating so loud I was sure Herbie could hear it in the next room. But instead of a long email there was just one line – a link to Mally's MySpace page. Oh God, was he going to dump me publicly?

It took for ever for the page to load up, but when it did, I saw that Mally had a new MySpace page. Instead of the old photo where he was wearing black and looking moody, this one had him in *my* T-shirt, the one I had made about global warming. At least that's what I thought it was at first. But when I looked closer I noticed that he'd changed the words. Instead of *Global warming is not cool* he'd put, *I'm sorry. It's cold without you, Lucy.* Then in brackets he'd put: *(shirts are useful!).* He must have altered the words on the computer. I gave a gulp.

Then the music started to play. It was Jeff Buckley; he had such a gorgeous voice, full of longing and melancholy. He was singing about love and pain and it made my whole body go goosebumpy. Mally had made this whole thing so that everyone could see it! Even his dad, though I doubt he logged on to MySpace much.

Mally really loved me. And I loved him. It was crazy to fight – a love like this only came along once in a lifetime. I grabbed my phone and punched in a text: *I'm sorry too. I love you. Meet in park? x*

I could see Mally waiting for me even before Socks and I turned the corner. He was always on time – that was one of his things. The flowerbeds were a riot of clashing colours but Mally, as ever, wore black. His shoulders were up by his ears and his hands were shoved deep into his pockets. But he still looked super-cute. I started to run, and so did Socks. Then Mally saw me and started running, so we probably looked like that cheesy advert where two people meet in the middle of a beach, only we were in Redworth gardens and we had a grey hairy terrier streaking between us. When we met we stopped short of hugging: it felt too much too soon. Socks obviously didn't feel the same way. He threw himself at Mally's legs like a hairy bomb.

'Ooomph! Hi, Socks!' He bent down and ruffled his head. I was glad that Socks was there to break the tension. 'How have you been, my old friend?'

'He's been OK. Actually he had a weird turn the other

day that I didn't tell you about.' Probably because I had so much else on my mind, I added silently.

'Yeah?'

'Yeah, he kind of went stiff and looked as if he was having a fit.'

'Oh no! Poor Socks.' Mally bent forward and kissed his head. 'Is he OK now?'

'Yeah, he's fine.'

'Good.' Mally stood up and looked at me. Jesus, the power of his eyes! Sometimes they were like laser beams.

'Listen, I am so sorry,' he said. 'About my dad. I should never have let him talk to you like that. Can you forgive me?'

'It's OK. I'm sorry too.'

'Did you log on to MySpace?'

'Yeah. It's the most romantic thing anyone's ever done for me. It was amazing.'

'Good. I love you. I meant every word. God, I hate my father. I hate him sometimes.'

'Don't say that. It's not your fault. It's fine. It's OK.' I stood on my tiptoes and kissed Mally very softly until he put his hands in my hair and pulled me tighter towards him. When I could hardly breathe we broke apart and stared at each other. Suddenly I laughed – it all seemed so ridiculous. Mally and I were meant to be together, end of story.

'What do you say we take a couple of hours off?' he said. 'We've been working so hard. We deserve it.'

'But what about your dad? I don't want a repeat of when we went to London. I mean, does he know you're even here?'

'Yes. I told him. I told him I was coming to see you.'

'And?'

'He has to put up with it. There's nothing he can do. Look, he'll come around in time. He'll understand how utterly wonderful you are. I promise.' Mally threw his arm around my neck and pulled me to his shoulder. His skin was lovely and smooth and warm.

'I just want to be with you,' I said into his neck. 'I don't care what we do. Let's do nothing.'

'We could take Socks for a walk,' said Mally, 'to this special place I know.'

'OK. But is it in the shade? Otherwise I'll just make freckles.'

'I'm crazy about your freckles,' said Mally. 'I wish *I* could make freckles.'

'It's not a skill exactly,' I said.

'Everything you do is clever. Don't be so down on yourself. You're amazing, and I want everyone to know.

LUCY BROOKS IS AMAZING!!'

'SHHH!' I said, embarrassed. 'The whole neighbour-hood will hear.'

'I don't care,' said Mally, taking in another deep breath. 'LUCY BROOKS IS AMA—'

I clamped my hand over his mouth and Mally took it away and kissed me again. Then he led me across the neatly clipped lawn where old people sat with their faces turned up to the sun and walked through the park, over the old railway line, until we were at last in a part of it that most people didn't visit. The grass had been mown recently, but somehow the wild flowers had grown back and were pushing through the hay in clouds of yellow and white. Butterflies flitted about and then the most random thing – when I lifted my eyes higher I could see tower blocks. We were in the town at the end of the universe.

It was perfect.

'Madam, allow me,' said Mally, taking off his jacket.

'Why thank you, kind gentleman,' I said. 'This will be just the protection for my young and tender flesh.'

'Your young and tender flesh,' said Mally, throwing himself down beside me and biting into my neck.

'Aaah, careful! I'll get a love bite and then everyone will laugh at me.' I tried to wriggle away from him. Socks started barking. 'Socks will protect me, won't you, Socks?'

'Socks will try and Socks will fail!' Mally threw his arm around the dog's neck. 'But don't you think everyone's laughing at me already, with my MySpace page?'

'What, is romance embarrassing?'

'You know what boys are like,' said Mally.

'You're not boys. You're different. That's why I love you.'

'You do love me, do you? I was worried for a second.' Mally looked at me with his enormous brown eyes.

'I hadn't gone off you, Mally. I just . . . realised I didn't know you as well as I thought.'

'You *do* know me, the real me. You know me better than anyone in the world. There are just some bits that you'd have to be in my skin to understand.'

'Any chance of that?' I said, snuggling closer.

'Maybe,' said Mally, smiling. Then we kissed for a very long time.

I knew Mally was trying to tell me to chill out, to accept that I could never totally know every little part of him, but that we could still be OK, but it scared me and I had to make a joke out of it.

Actually, Mally was right – I did know the real him. He knew the real me too, the part of me that not even my mum knew. It was scary. I felt as if I was on the threshold of growing up, of starting a whole new life. But a little part of me wanted to hold back, to cling to what I knew: it felt safer. I didn't tell Mally though, and if I'd thought about it, that was a little part of me *he'd* never know either.

'What d'you think we'll be when we grow up?' I said. 'Isn't it mind-blowing to think that soon we'll have jobs and cars and *everything*?'

'I *am* grown up. I'm eighteen, remember? And just about to embark on a great career as a . . .' Mally paused. 'I don't know what. Something useful. I'll need a job before I get to uni, to add to my CV.'

Wow. Mally was right, of course. Sometimes it blew my mind how sorted he was. But I guess, from the outside, I was grown-up too. Although inside I sometimes still felt like a kid. I couldn't imagine leaving home and setting up on my own. But I wouldn't have to, not yet.

'You, what d'you want to be?' Mally asked. 'A fashion designer?'

'Or a textile designer, or, I dunno,' I said.

'You should really go for it, you know? You're really good. You have so much talent.'

'You're a lovely boyfriend,' I said. I wished I hadn't brought up the future. I knew Mally was going off to uni at the end of the year and we hadn't talked about how – or if – we would make it work. I didn't know how I could compete against all those hot student chicks. But I couldn't face asking him about it now. We were lying in the shade of a willow tree; Socks was snuffling about in the grass. Mally had his arm underneath my neck. I stared up through the branches at the blue sky. Everything was good. On this perfect blue morning, I didn't want us to be anything. I just wanted us to be. Together.

Chapter 9

♥

When exams finally happened I enjoyed them, in a weird kind of way. I mean, obviously they were incredibly stressful, but there was something satisfying about concentrating really hard and coming out knowing I'd done my best. There was the occasional bummer – like chemistry – where I sat there hot and flustered not knowing what the hell to do. When I came out of that one I knew I hadn't done very well, but no surprises there. It was also quite difficult after the end of one exam to have to pick up my books and straight away start cramming for the next.

But, one by one, I could cross the dreaded dates off my calendar, until there was one more – English lit – which wasn't too bad except for a question or two . . . and then *no more*. No more GCSEs!!!! I could cut my work up and throw it into the fire if I wanted. Except that I didn't – it seemed like bad karma.

Mally finished later than me. He had fewer exams, but

each one was so much more important. After most of them he seemed pretty pleased, but after the second economics exam he came out looking dejected. I tried to cheer him up but he said he'd messed up. None of the questions he'd been expecting were on the paper and then he'd panicked and answered the wrong ones. By the time he realised, it was too late to start again. I guess he had so much riding on the results he probably felt nothing was good enough. I knew he was a genius. To get into Cambridge he had to get three A's. His teachers had told him that he'd get them, but they were pretty high marks even so.

Now there was nothing but two long months of summer holidays, which by rights should have been mine and Mally's to spend as we pleased. The only problem was that Mum had booked a holiday in Spain for *two weeks*. She'd been saving up for it for ages and I knew I should be pleased, but I wasn't. It would mean two precious weeks away from Mally.

But first we had a week of parties and I was definitely looking forward to *that*. Mally's friends' parties were the real deal: lots of them were going to university at the end of the year and some were taking a year off to travel. It was so weird to think that next year they'd all be gone and Rachel and I would be in the sixth form. Everything was changing. Normally I love change; I can't wait to be grown-up and make a start on life. But now, holding on to Mally's hand as he chatted away to all his friends I realised that these last few months had been the most amazing of my life. Why would I want anything to change – what could possibly get better?

Mally sure as hell could dance. He wasn't one of those arm-flailers or leg-tremblers that it was dangerous to get too close to, and believe me there were enough of those in this town. Mally snaked his hips around in a figure of eight and made this little shimmy with his shoulders that I had tried (and failed) to copy because it was just so damn sexy. Sometimes he twirled me around under his arm and out in front and around behind until I was dizzy and breathless. I felt as if we were the coolest couple on the dance floor, which made me self-conscious and proud at the same time.

But ironically it was the party that should have been the most fun of all that turned out to be the party from hell. I had arranged to meet Rachel and Ian there, and Mally had called up Raj too. It was at a friend's house that we all knew, and Mally had said that he was getting in a massive sound system.

Sure enough, when we arrived, music was pumping out of what, in a previous existence, had been the sitting room. Rachel and Ian were in the VIP room – formerly known as the kitchen. This was the first time we'd double dated – I'd suggested it a few times but Rachel hadn't seemed keen. She kept saying Ian was busy, was with his mates, or down the pub. At this party though, all his mates were there, the South End Crew and, to be honest, they weren't doing wonders for the atmosphere. They stood around in a big baggy-trousered group. They had their backs to everyone and were grasping beer cans in their fists like they were pumping weights. Occasionally one of them swaggered over to the dance floor and pulled a couple of moves that he'd obviously learned from MTV. Then the others hooted at him and punched the air. Rachel stood with Mally and me more than with them, though every so often Ian would come strutting over and run his hands all over her.

I have to say I could see why Rachel hadn't wanted to double date. Ian wasn't one of her best boyfriends – and she'd had some bad ones. Rachel did seem a bit embarrassed and kept backing away from Ian, but he wasn't having any of it.

'Yo babycakes, whassup? You don wanna party?'

'I don't think you've met my friends. Lucy and Mally. And this is Raj,' said Rachel, reversing and turning to face us all.

Ian glanced in our direction. 'Howz it hangin. Listen, superstar, wot you say we fine somewhere more soothin? Me and my mates is thinkin of chippin and I thought yeah we could like go back to your place and chill, innit?'

Raj rolled his eyes.

'Oh, I don't think so,' said Rachel. 'My parents will wait up for me and well . . .' She trailed off.

'I getcha.' Ian's eyes looked glazed and his breath smelled of beer. 'But if it's jus us two, yeah, they ain't gonna have no beef.'

'Well, umm, they might.'

'All right, superstar, whatever, yeah? We can talk about this la'er. Let's dance, yeah?'

'I could do with putting out a few moves on the floor myself,' said Raj to Mally. 'Not with that moron though.'

Mally nodded. But I felt bad abandoning Rachel, especially when she was pointing to a spot beside her on the dance floor. 'Do you mind if I go over?' I said.

'Then we'll all go over,' said Mally.

It was then that it happened. We heard voices shout really loud over the music towards us.

'Hey, Ian, mate. Wot you doing dancing with those Pakis?'

All the blood left my face. Had those idiots really said

that? But they had – I could hear them laughing. Ian smiled stupidly. He didn't say anything.

'Ian!' said Rachel, pulling away from him. 'What are your mates *like*? That's totally out of order! Aren't you going to make them apologise?'

'For what, superstar? You ain't gonna let a bit of loose talk ruin our night, is you?' Ian grabbed at Rachel's hand.

I looked at Mally. I knew he'd heard because his face had a blank look that I'd never seen before. I felt a surge of anger. 'Oh my God, Mally, those *bloody idiots*!' I said. 'I'm going to —'

'Don't worry about it,' Mally said in a flat voice. 'It's nothing I haven't heard before.'

'But I want to just go over and —'

'What's the point?' said Mally.

'Yeah. Let's just go,' said Raj. Raj looked totally unlike himself. His face was closed tight, like a fist. But he started to walk out with his head down.

'But they shouldn't, they shouldn't just get away with it!' I shouted.

'Listen, Lucy,' Mally hissed. 'There's about ten of them and two of us.'

'And me and Rachel!'

'Don't be so stupid. Raj and I are the ones they have the beef with – and you are girls. And if we get aggro they'll beat us *all* up. I know their type. Raj is right. We're going.'

I was so furious I hadn't noticed what was going on with Rachel, but as we went to walk out she was right there in front of us, without Ian.

'I'm so sorry, Mally, Raj,' she said, totally flustered.

As we passed by the South End Crew I let Mally, Raj and Rachel go on ahead. But I couldn't walk by without saying something. 'If you think that being racist is cool, you're wrong. Why are you dressing up like black kids when you're all white? You bunch of utter *wankers*.' I said the last word quite quietly, but I stretched it out and I was sure they could all hear me because everyone had stopped talking.

Mally appeared at the door. 'What the hell are you doing? Do you want to get us all beaten up? *Come on.*'

He grabbed me by the arm and pulled me out. I knew he was right, but I was still glad I'd said something.

On the way home, Rachel kept apologising to Mally. Raj was unusually quiet. It was quite a long walk home and Rachel and Mally drew ahead of us. I could hear her explaining that she hadn't been seeing Ian for long, hardly knew him in fact. Mally was giving short one-word answers, but Rachel didn't seem to be able to let it go.

Love Divided

Raj and I were left walking together. I didn't know what to say to Raj at the best of times, let alone now. I felt awful. At least I had managed to say something to those tossers, and maybe made them think about what they'd said. On the other hand, maybe they were too drunk and stupid to think about anything, and maybe I'd been lucky the South End Crew hadn't come chasing after us.

'I'm really sorry about all that. They were complete losers,' I said in the end.

'I know. It's not your fault,' Raj said.

After another long pause I said, 'I mean, maybe I can understand a little bit. Mr Khan, he doesn't like me, because I'm white. Mally must have told you.'

'He did tell me. He was pretty embarrassed, and it's horrible. It's nothing to do with you, you know that, right? Mr Khan is a difficult old bugger.'

I nodded.

After a pause Raj continued: 'What you said about understanding: you're right in a way. You've known what it's like, once. But Mally and I, we have to go through this all the time. We never know when it's going to come up.'

I blushed furiously. I knew what Raj meant. I thought about the time when Mally and I had been in the café. I had sat down first, but when Mally joined me, these two women nearby looked at him and really obviously picked up their handbags and put them on their laps. And to think I had thought I was in a similar predicament with my red hair!

'I'm, I'm sorry,' I stammered.

'It's OK, I know you mean well.'

We were silent again. Once again I was beginning to wonder whether I understood Mally as well as I'd thought.

Rachel and Mally had stopped outside Rachel's house. Rachel gave me an uncomfortable half-smile and looked as if she was going to say something, but she didn't. She just shoved her hands in her pockets and went inside. I went over to Mally and put my arm around his waist. I could feel his ribs pressing through his T-shirt, but even as close to me as that, I knew that he was still miles away.

Soon we reached Raj's front door. He and Mally embraced.

'See ya later, bro,' said Raj, patting him on the back.

'Later,' said Mally.

Then it was just Mally and me. I felt as if a chasm had opened up between us and to try to stop it I took his hand and squeezed it tight. 'Are you OK?' I said.

'I'm fine,' he said. But I knew he wasn't, and neither was I.

'It doesn't mean anything, those kids . . .' I said.

'It means what it means,' said Mally.

His voice was hard, and distant. I hadn't heard him use that tone before. We lapsed into silence. The sound of our shoes on the pavement was as loud as gun cracks.

Eventually we reached my house. I hugged Mally tight, I wanted to keep him with me for a few minutes longer, and for one instant I felt Mally relax and rest his head on my shoulder. Then he tensed again and moved away from me. I wished I had never let him go.

After that I had to go to Spain. Even though Mally said I should enjoy myself, and that he wished he could go too, he *wasn't* going too, and I knew it would be hard to enjoy myself without him.

Even before I left, Mally was really busy. He'd got a job as an intern in a company that organised car pooling in the local area. Mally had to contact people and convince them to take part. I just knew he'd be great at it – I remembered how passionate he'd been at the debate – but it meant he was at work all day. As well as that, three evenings a week he had to help out in his dad's restaurant.

When I did see Mally it wasn't nearly as easy as it had been – we hardly ever laughed any more. Don't get me wrong, we were still in love. I loved Mally painfully. But since the party he'd been distant, almost as if he was still at work, or somewhere else completely. Then I'd ask him what he was thinking, even though I knew he hated that question. He'd just say, 'Nothing'. But it is impossible to think *nothing*: everybody is thinking of something, even if it's just door knobs and fried eggs.

The worst thing was that Mum had made a real effort with the holiday. She'd got us a nice hotel near the Ramblas in Barcelona, right in the middle of all the action. Herbie was over the moon; there were so many crazy street-performers, he would probably have been happy spending the whole two weeks watching fire-eaters on stilts.

The weather was boiling hot too, just what I usually love (though I have to slap on factor 50 the whole time), and Mum let us go to the beach rather than drag us round museums. And I did try, I really did, to enjoy myself, but all I could think about was Mally.

Mally Mally Mally Mally Mally.

How it would have all been so much better if he were here. How sexy he would have looked in a pair of swimming trunks. How we could have run into the sea and frolicked in the waves.

I reached my arm across the towel and checked my

mobile again. He still hadn't texted. The last text I'd got was the previous morning and I'd sent him three texts since then. He must be really busy at work. Oh God, how was I going to manage nine more days without him? The day after next it'd be a week till we went home. Then I'd be halfway through . . .

Mum broke into my thoughts. 'Do you want me to keep your mobile in my bag? Seems a bit hot out in the sun.'

'No, it's OK.'

There was a silence.

'You'd better make sure you cover up well. The sun is very strong out here.'

'Yes, Mum, I know.'

There was another silence.

'How about going into the sea? You haven't gone in since you arrived,' said Mum.

I squinted across at her. She was wearing a tattered old straw hat she'd pulled out of the cupboard at home at the last minute and a horrible, loud swimsuit she'd probably had since the Seventies. I suddenly felt incredibly annoyed.

'Look, I don't want to go into the poxy sea, OK? Stop hassling me. I just want to be left alone.'

Mum's face hardened. 'Fine, Lucinda,' she said, getting

up and packing her bag. 'Be like that. Just stay here stewing for as long as you like. You've been absolutely miserable ever since we arrived, and to tell you the truth I'm getting sick of it. I'm off to get an ice-cream. Coming, Herbie?'

Herbie shot me a bewildered look and followed Mum, scuffing sand on to my leg as he went.

Great. Peace at last. I slotted my headphones into my ears and scrolled down to Jeff Buckley. He understood what I was going through. I listened to the whole album with tears in my eyes, my heart soaring up above the sea. It was only when I began to trudge back up the beach towards the hotel that I started to think about Mum. Maybe she had the tiniest fraction of a point...I probably hadn't been the greatest holiday companion so far. But I couldn't help it! I *was* trying. I could hear Mum's voice in my head: *Yes, very trying!* Maybe I should try harder ...

Forty-five minutes later, after I'd got lost a couple of times, I finally showed up at the hotel. Mum was in the lobby with a cup of tea.

'Look, Mum, I'm sorry,' I said. 'I know I've been miserable to have around.' As soon as I started to speak a lump came into my throat.

Mum beckoned for me to sit down next to her. 'I just

want you to make a bit more of an effort, darling, for Herbie if not for me.'

'I just miss Mally so much!'

'I know, but you'll see him in a week!'

'I just . . . I don't know . . . he hasn't texted . . . and I hardly see him even when I *am* at home, and I love him so much, you know?'

'Lucy,' Mum gave me a squeeze, 'Mally is a very nice boy. And he's your first love and it's a hugely important thing. I just wish, for your sake, that the relationship could be a little smoother. First love should be pure and joyful and, I don't know, lovely.'

'It *is* pure and joyful! It's just that sometimes the world gets in the way.'

'Yes, well, if you love each other enough, I'm sure you'll find a path through it.' Mum smiled at me encouragingly. 'Well, I'm glad we've had this chat.'

'So am I. Thanks, Mum. I'll try to be better, I promise.' As I said it, I felt just like a little girl.

The second week of the holiday was much better. I had to be very strict with my mind and not let it wander off down Avenue Mally, but when I put a roadblock on any thoughts that were going that way, I found myself having some fun – Barcelona was a really cool place.

Even so, it was great to be back. As soon as I saw Mally I threw myself into his arms.

'Whoa! Lucy! Hey – how are you?' he said, as I smothered him with kisses in the hallway.

'God, I missed you so much, Mally! I didn't know it was possible. I thought of you every day.' I was going to say, every hour, every minute, but I could feel myself sounding a bit mad, so I didn't.

'I missed you too.'

'Did you? Did you really? You weren't too busy at work?'

'What do you mean – too busy to miss you? I *was* busy, but that didn't mean I didn't think of you. I thought of you all the time.'

'It's just that sometimes you didn't text. You're OK, right?'

'Yeah. I'm fine!' Mally stepped back. 'How was your holiday? Meet any nice men?'

'*As if!* I missed you so crazily I didn't even see any other men.'

We went to my room and snuggled together on my bed. It was fantastic to feel his arms around me again and his lips on mine and his hands in my hair and the weight of his body on top of mine. I felt like I'd died and gone to heaven.

But then Mally turned over and lay on his back, staring at the ceiling.

'Are you OK?' I asked, stroking his hair.

'I'm fine. I'm so glad you're back – I mean it. I'm just, well, I can't help thinking about my exam results.'

'Oh, Mally. I know you'll do well. You're a genius.'

'I've just got so much riding on it.'

'I know, baby. Don't worry,' I said, smoothing his brow. 'How can I take your mind off it?'

'I mean, if I don't get three A's, I'm screwed.'

'How about *this*?' I kissed his nose.

'And Dad'll be totally gutted too.'

'Or this?' I kissed his eyes.

'Mmmm.'

'Or this?' I brought my lips down on his and gave him a full-on snog. Finally Mally reacted, putting both his hands on my bum and squeezing it. Bingo!

It was good to see I could still work some of the old Lucy magic.

Chapter 10

♥

When I woke up the next day it was raining again. I could hear it beating down on my window pane – it had been raining for a solid week. Some people were saying it was because of global warming. It seemed like any kind of weird weather was blamed on global warming. I thought of Mally, already working away at his office. He was helping out at the restaurant tonight, so I probably wouldn't see him then either.

With a big sigh I got up, pulled my dressing gown over my pyjamas and went downstairs. Thank goodness Herbie was at a friend's today and I could have the house to myself.

It wasn't until I'd made myself a cup of tea that I noticed Socks was still in his basket. Normally he would have struggled up to meet me, even though his joints were stiff. Something was wrong. I went over to him. He was trembling like he was cold, but it was really warm in the kitchen. He had froth at the corner of his mouth.

My heart gave a great leap of fear.

'MUM! COME QUICK! SOCKS IS HAVING ANOTHER FIT!'

'It's OK, Socks,' I said to him as I stroked his head. He barely seemed to recognise me.

'MUM!!!'

Mum appeared at the door and took in the scene immediately. 'Let's get him to the vet. Now!'

We laid a blanket on the back seat for Socks and drove as fast as we could. 'I was afraid of this,' Mum said.

'What do you mean?'

'This. Those little fits he had before,' said Mum.

'But they were ages ago! He's completely recovered since then,' I said.

'He had another while we were away. Mrs Karposhki said.'

'Why didn't you tell me?' I looked at Mum in astonishment.

'I didn't know how serious it was, darling. I didn't want to worry you, and you were so involved with Mally. I'm sorry, I should have.'

I was sitting in the back, with Socks's head on my knee. He'd stopped shaking now, but he was very limp. He turned his eyes towards me and attempted to lick my hand. Darling Socks! Even though he was so ill, he still wanted to provide me with reassurance.

It seemed like an age that we were sitting in the vet's waiting room, but I lost all sense of time; I was just hugging Socks close to my chest and comforting him, as if by sheer force of willpower I could make him be OK. I texted Mally at one point: *Please call. Socks ill!!* But Mally didn't reply, or at least I don't think he did, because then the vet showed up and what followed next was a bit of a blur.

We laid Socks on the table and he looked so old and fragile I started crying immediately, even before the vet said anything. The vet checked him over and asked a few questions. Had he been drinking a lot recently? Mum said, yes, he had. Then the vet looked at his gums and seemed to sigh.

'And he's been having these fits?' she said.

'For quite a while,' I said, shooting a glance at Mum.

'But today is the worst?'

'Yes.'

'And he's how old?'

'We don't know exactly,' said Mum. 'Probably about twelve or thirteen.'

'Yes, that's quite old for a small dog,' said the vet, patting him gently. Then she looked up at us with a grim expression. 'I'm afraid this is going to be very hard to hear. But I believe Socks has renal failure.'

I looked at her blankly.

'His kidneys have given out. Now, I'm going to take some blood, to make absolutely sure. The results should be ready tomorrow.'

'But can you fix him?' I said.

'I very much doubt it,' said the vet. 'Given his age. I'm very sorry.'

Mum and I took Socks home and we made a nest for him in the living room. He was still really weak and wouldn't eat anything. His breath smelled weird, though I didn't care. I lay down next to him. I was sending messages up to God: *If you let Socks be OK, I'll never go shopping instead of taking him on a walk again!* My brain wasn't working properly, all my thoughts were disjointed and as soon as I said something I forgot what it was. I suddenly remembered Mum should be at work.

'I took the day off,' said Mum.

I still couldn't believe it. When I woke up this morning, everything was fine. Now this. I sent another message to God: *If you let him be OK I'll never leave him alone again!*

Mally called.

'Mally, it's awful! He's just all weird. Like, I don't know, like it's not really him. This all feels like some kind of horrible dream,' I said. 'The vet says it's renal failure.'

'Poor little dog,' said Mally. 'I'm so sorry, Lucy. What happened?'

I told him, and how I felt so bad we'd left him when we went to Spain, and all the times since I'd got back that I hadn't taken him for a walk because he and I had been together.

'It's not your fault, sweetheart,' said Mally. 'The vet told you Socks was old, didn't she?'

'I guess so.'

'Well then, when people, or dogs, get old they get prone to all sorts of things. It might just be Socks's time.'

'Time for what?'

'Time to go.'

I began to cry. 'I don't want him to go!'

'I know you don't, sweetheart.'

Then the phone went muffled and I could hear Mally speaking to someone else. He came back on the line.

'Look, I'm really sorry, Lucy, but I'm going to have to go.'

I was silent. I had been hoping that he could leave work and come over.

'I'm really tied up in here, I'm sorry. I'll call you as soon as I can.'

'You can't leave work early and come round?' I said.

'I can't, I've got so much on. I'm really sorry, sweetheart. Then I've got to go straight to the restaurant. I just . . . I don't see how I can fit it in.'

I looked at poor Socks again. His eyes were closed, he seemed hardly to be breathing. My heart was made of lead. 'OK. Whatever. I just really needed to see you.' I was desperate for comfort and all I wanted was his arms around me.

'Sorry, Lucy,' he said again. 'I'll go into work late tomorrow, OK? I promise. But let's speak later.'

As Mally put the phone down Mum came in carrying a tray. 'How is he?' she mouthed.

'He can't come round,' I said.

'Who d'you mean, Socks?' said Mum anxiously. 'Has he lost consciousness?'

'No, I mean Mally. He's busy at the restaurant.'

'Oh, OK.' Mum put the tray down at my feet.

'Oh God, Mum, I wish he was here and I wish Socks was OK!' I started crying again. I knew I sounded like a baby.

'Oh, darling.' She wrapped both her arms around me. 'I know. It's very hard. I know how much you love Socks. And Mally too, come to that.'

I could feel my bottom lip wobbling and then, I couldn't stop them, tears just started falling down my cheeks. 'Socks can't die! I've had him, I've had him since I was a kid! He's grown up with me! He's like my brother!'

Mum held me until I stopped crying.

'I don't want to leave him tonight. Is that OK?'

'Of course, darling.'

I curled my body round his small furry one. Socks felt small and defenceless. My heart was so heavy it felt as if it was falling straight through my ribcage. I couldn't imagine life without Socks. He was probably the creature who'd been through most with me in the entire world. Without him I'd be all alone.

It was awful breaking the news to Herbie. Even though Socks was really my dog, Herbie loved him and he was just a kid. I watched him trying to take it all in; he took his glasses off and rubbed his eyes very hard.

'Is he going to die?' he said.

'We don't know,' I said. 'He might.'

Herbie burst into tears and rushed over to Mum for a hug.

During the night I kept dreaming Socks was fine, but then I'd wake up and it was like finding out all over again. He had another fit in the middle of the night, his back arching against me and his eyes rolling back in his head.

By the morning I was exhausted. As soon as the office opened Mum phoned the vet. When she put the phone down her expression was grim. 'It's what she thought. His kidneys aren't working.'

When I heard her say that I wondered how I could ever have hoped she'd say anything different.

'What can we do?'

'The vet says that the kindest thing would be to put him down. Otherwise he might live for another week or so, but he'd be in a lot of pain.'

I looked over at Socks and I knew she was right. He seemed to be pleading with me. 'OK.'

I needed Mally so much right now, but when I called him it went straight to voice mail. He couldn't be at work already! He'd promised! Did he have any idea what I was going through?

In the end Mum, Herbie and I went down to the vet's together. I sat with Socks on my lap. Mum had her arms round me. She was crying, which set me off really badly.

'It won't hurt Socks at all, I promise you,' said the vet. 'I'll give him this injection, then he'll drift off to sleep.'

I was stroking Socks's head and telling him everything was OK. That he could let go now, that he didn't need to stay around for us. I felt Socks go all floppy, as if he was finally relaxed. Then his breathing stopped. Just at that moment I felt a tingle in the palm of my hands. Later I thought that perhaps it was his spirit rushing up towards heaven.

It had all happened so quickly. I could never take anything for granted again.

Mally was waiting for me when we got home. But it was too late. Socks was dead. I put him in a box that I'd filled with his favourite things: his old ball, his favourite treats and his lead. Mum and I and Herbie stood around while Mally dug a hole at the bottom of the garden. I said a prayer, which I'd written earlier, about how Socks had helped me grow up, but now his duty was over and he was better off in dog heaven. The fields were greener there and there were plenty of rabbits to chase. I didn't know if I actually believed in dog heaven but I couldn't deal with the fact that Socks had just vanished. Then I put him in the ground and scattered some earth over him. Mally gave me a giant hug but it didn't really help. I was still devastated.

Chapter 11

On the day I knew Mally would be getting his results I called him early in the morning. His mobile went straight to voice mail – was that good or bad? Either he was celebrating or too upset to answer. Over the next hour I must have called Mally thirty times – I know he must have seen my name come up and I know I shouldn't have kept phoning, but I was possessed by some weird phone weevil. I just couldn't stop my finger from pressing redial. As the minutes wore on and still he didn't pick up, or phone me, I began to get a bad feeling. The feeling grew worse and worse until I was convinced that Mally had committed suicide. Which is why, when he finally phoned me back, I was happy just to hear his voice and I didn't realise at first what he was saying.

'I didn't get into Cambridge.'

'Oh God, no! But surely they can't . . . What did you get?'

'Two A's and a B.'

'But you're so close, couldn't you talk to them?'

'Talk to them! Don't be stupid.'

'Oh, OK, but . . .'

'I failed, Lucy. That's all there is to it.'

'But, Mally, you didn't fail. Your results are great. *You're* great. Look, let's meet up – where shall we meet?'

'I can't meet, Lucy, not right now. We'll talk soon, yeah?'

And just like that, he cut me off.

Mally didn't phone me that day. Or the next. Or the next or the next. A week passed and still I heard nothing. I texted him, I phoned him, I emailed him, I MSNed him. Nothing. So I went to look for him. I went to all the places we used to go: the café, the river, the school playing fields, the park with the tower blocks. Come to think of it, there was hardly anywhere Mally and I had not been together. The whole town was one big painful memory of him. Even though I'd grown up here, it was as if when I was with Mally I truly saw everything.

The only place I didn't go to was his house. I hovered around the bottom of his street for a while, then I walked past his house, craning my head to see if he was inside. Over the next couple of days I walked up and down quite a few times, feeling more and more like a stalker, but the house just sat there, its bay windows looking like puffed-out cheeks blowing me away.

Once or twice I walked past the restaurant. The first time there were just a few people having lunch. The second time must have been in the lull between lunch and dinner because the place was deserted. I was just about to walk away when I noticed a figure sitting in the back. He looked like Mally for a second and my heart lurched. But it wasn't Mally. It was his dad. He hadn't seen me; his head was in his hands. There was something about the slump of his shoulders and the press of his head into his palms that looked . . . well . . . totally dejected. As if he would sit in that chair and never get up. I almost, for a moment, felt sorry for him. Then I walked on: it would be a nightmare if Mr Khan saw me staring in at him through the window.

After that I sat indoors with Herbie, just to be near my computer in case Mally felt like sending me a message. I missed Socks so badly. Comforting me was what he was best at. Herbie and I played computer games; usually I hate computer games but it was just the kind of mindless activity I needed. Herbie was thrashing me as usual.

'I wish Ehsan was here. He's so much better than you at this,' Herbie said.

'Thanks a lot, Herbie,' I said. 'Where is Ehsan anyway?'

'I dunno. I haven't seen him.'

'What do you mean?'

'I mean, I haven't seen him. Not for a month.'

'A *month*? That's a long time. Why?'

'He's not allowed.'

'What do you mean?' I was shocked.

'He emailed me and said he wasn't allowed to come round any more.'

'But . . . why?'

'He didn't say,' said Herbie. 'He just said there were loads of rows at home.'

I sat there in a state of numb shock. It was obviously because of Mally and me. But why the hell hadn't Mally told me about any of this? Didn't he tell me *anything* about his life? Then I felt furious. How bloody dare Mr Khan stop the friendship of two kids?

Herbie was looking at me weirdly. 'Why have you gone red?' he asked.

'I'm just feeling hot, Herb. I'm sorry about Ehsan. Do you miss him?'

'Yeah,' said Herbie. 'He was my friend.'

I put my arms round him and gave him a big hug. I don't know if he felt better. I certainly didn't.

My results were OK, although probably not by Mally's

standards. I got an A in fashion and textile design, an A in English literature and a few others. Apart from that it was B's and C's. The horrible thing was that normally I would have been super-pleased, but with everything that was going on, I still felt gutted.

Mum went to work and came back again to find me still sitting in the same place. She was really sweet; I thought she'd get at me about doing my chores. I hardly ate a thing even though Mum cooked my favourite meals. She didn't usually have time to cook, but she served spaghetti bolognaise, or roast chicken, and it would smell great but I just wasn't hungry. I kept thinking how Socks would have loved all the extra food. Come to think of it, Mum must have left work early to have the time to roast a chicken. Herbie couldn't believe his luck.

I hadn't really told Mum what was going on with Mally. Actually I hadn't really told anyone. Rachel had gone away for a few days to a family thing, and I knew if I started telling anyone else I would begin to cry and not be able to stop. But one evening, after I'd pushed yet another delicious dinner around my plate without eating any of it, Mum asked me if there was anything I wanted to talk about. She looked so concerned and sweet that I started to cry. And then it all came out. How it had been my fault that Mally hadn't got into Cambridge and that

I'd ruined his life. Now he was punishing me by blanking me. How Mr Khan would hate me even more. And how things had been going downhill since the party.

Mum sat next to me on the sofa with both her arms around me. Eventually I stopped speaking and was just sobbing into her chest like I hadn't done since I was a little girl. This voice in my head was saying, *This just isn't fun any more.* When I heard the voice I cried even harder.

Mum wiped away my tears with her thumb. 'Darling Lucy. You've got to stop blaming yourself. This is nothing to do with you. I *know* he doesn't think you ruined his life. You both worked really hard.'

'We did work hard, Mum. We did.'

'Two A's and a B is hardly a poor result.'

'It's not enough for Cambridge.'

'I expect he'll survive,' said Mum.

'I love him so much.'

'I know you do, darling. And first love, well, there's nothing quite like it. I just wish you could have had an easier time with it. Perhaps a boy from a more straightforward family.'

I looked up at her. 'If by straightforward you mean white I —'

'Of course not, darling! I mean that there're so many

other factors at play here. You could love and love each other, but sometimes . . . well . . . love is not enough.'

'What do you mean?'

'Darling. I loved your father as much as you love Mally. I loved him so much I thought my heart would burst. And d'you know what? It *was* enough, in the beginning. When you kids were both very young I felt as if there was no man in the world I'd rather be with. I felt that he understood me in a way no one else ever would.'

'That's exactly how I feel!'

Mum was talking to me as a grown-up. She had never spoken to me like this before. I felt suddenly taller, as if by just speaking to me this way she had actually made me grow up, there and then.

'I know, and it's wonderful.' Mum gave my shoulder a squeeze. 'That feeling carried your father and me through the birth of two children. Even when things started to get bad, I kept hoping for a return of the good times. I tried to ignore the warning signs, when your father would stay out late at the pub and come home drunk. The bottle of red wine after he came home from work.'

'What are you saying, Mum? Mally is hardly an alcoholic. He doesn't even drink.'

'I'm just saying that, even though I loved your dad as much as I did, I couldn't make it work. He had something else that was more important to him, and that was alcohol.'

'And now his new family,' I said, sounding bitter, even though I didn't mean to.

'Oh, Lucy,' said my mum. 'You know what? Your father *will* come back to you and Herbie. For the moment your dad has just replaced the drink with his new wife – I'm sure he loves her, but she's become everything and he can't see beyond her. Maybe, for no reason of your own, you and Herbie remind him of the time when he was still drinking.' Mum paused. 'But I know your father. He is actually a good man, believe it or not. He loves you and he will come back to you. But I know you miss him and I'm sorry.'

Mum gave me a huge hug. When we pulled apart I saw that she had tears in her eyes.

I hadn't let myself admit, except that first time with Mally, that I did really miss my dad. Every time I thought about him it was as if I slammed a door on the thought and locked it up somewhere in my head. It had seemed easier that way. But now Mum had brought it out into the open I felt a lot better. Especially if what she said was right, that Dad would come back into our lives.

'Thanks, Mum. I do miss him sometimes, but I've got you.'

'And I've got you.'

We hugged, a bit tearily.

'But . . . I still don't see how Mally is like Dad.'

'Mally is not really like your father. But in one way he is – they both have something else they love as much, if not more, than us.'

'What do you mean? Mally loves me! He's told me so a thousand times.'

'I know he loves you, darling. I'm sure he loves you very much. But does he love you enough?'

I stared at Mum angrily.

'He hasn't called you at all this week,' she said, very gently.

'He's been upset! His father is probably giving him hell. Maybe he can't.'

'But if you were upset, isn't Mally the first person you would call?' Mum said.

'Yeah, but it's different for him.'

'Different?'

'Obviously!' I was bright red. 'He's got, you know, a different family from me. A different culture, more responsibilities. Plus, of course, his dad is a horrible old man who hates me. He's probably taken his mobile away.' As crazy as it sounds, I had had that thought this week.

'But there are plenty of other ways to get in touch, darling, aren't there?' said Mum.

'Maybe . . .' I had had *that* thought too. 'But our relationship is so much more difficult for him than it is for me. Did you know Mr Khan has stopped Ehsan from coming round here because of Mally and me?'

'I noticed he hadn't been round lately. But I didn't know why. That's terrible,' said Mum. 'Poor Herbie.'

'So now you know how horrible Mr Khan is. It's no wonder Mally hasn't called. There's been loads of rows about us at Mally's house. Herbie's told me. Mally must have stood up for me to his dad.'

'I'm sure he did, darling. I'm not saying Mally doesn't love you. But what about when Socks died – it wasn't his dad who stopped him coming over then, was it?'

'You never know! I mean, it's such a different culture. His dad hates dogs! Anyway,' I added, 'Mally was there at the funeral!'

'Darling, I'm just playing Devil's Advocate. I only want to see you happy. And these last few weeks you haven't been happy at all.'

'Yes I have!' I shouted, even though I hadn't.

'The point of being with somebody you love is that you *share* things with them,' said Mum gently. 'Bad things as well as good. Recently you seem to have been going through an awful lot on your own.'

'We do share things! He understands me, and I understand him!' I was hating this conversation – it was like having my insides stirred about by a hot poker.

'I know you do. But...well...you don't share *experiences* all that much. Mally just isn't around. He's very busy, and motivated, which is great. But if he doesn't have time for you now, what will happen when he goes to university?'

I was silent. I had had the exact same thoughts. But it was horrible to hear them out loud coming from someone else.

'I wouldn't have said anything, darling, but I've been watching you these last few weeks and I just want to try to help you. You've been putting your whole life on hold for Mally. But would he do the same for you? You can tell me to mind my own business if you like. But perhaps the whole reason that you've been so obsessed with Mally is because you can feel him drawing back.'

My head was throbbing. That kind of made sense. If he'd only called me this last week I wouldn't have gone so crazy.

'Perhaps Mally has been avoiding you,' Mum continued gently, 'not because of Mr Khan – after all, as you say, Mally *did* stand up to him and he knows his own mind. Perhaps he just doesn't *want* to call.'

'You *are* saying he doesn't love me,' I said miserably. Just saying those words cut my mouth to pieces.

'No, I'm not. He does love you,' said Mum, taking my hand and squeezing it very tight. 'Just maybe not as much as you love him.'

Oh God, this was horrible. Horrible. I started to cry again. Recently I seemed to have spent my whole life in tears. 'But why? What's so wrong with me? Am I not good enough?'

'Don't ever say that!' said Mum fiercely. 'This is not about your worth. This is about Mally. Have you heard the saying, "what does not destroy me makes me stronger"? '

'No . . . I don't like the sound of it.'

'What it means is that when you come through all of this – and I know it feels like you never will, but you *will* – you'll be so much stronger than you are now.'

'That wouldn't be hard,' I said.

'Don't say that. You are lovely. You are the very best daughter I could have ever wished for. I love you.'

'Thanks, Mum.'

But nothing could make me feel better. I couldn't stop crying. Some of the things she had said I had been thinking already, only in a secret part of my brain that I hadn't really allowed myself to see. Some of the things I hadn't let myself admit.

But I wasn't ready to give up on Mally yet.

I had to see him again and see if Mum was right.

Chapter 12

♥

Thoughts of Mally wound round my brain like a long piece of barbed wire. I couldn't sleep properly and, when I finally did fall asleep, I was so restless and I dreamed about exactly the same stuff that I spent my time obsessing over during the day, so that I never knew if I was dreaming or awake. After such a long time without hearing from Mally he had grown into more of an idea than a reality. In my dreams he'd at first seem the same Mally that I had fallen in love with, but then he'd turn around and I'd discover he was actually a robot, or he'd be made of glass and crack into a thousand tiny pieces.

So it's fair to say that when he finally texted, ten days after his results had come through, I wasn't as pleased as I'd originally thought I would be. It wasn't lost on me that he'd *texted* either, not even a proper phone call. But I wanted to meet him. I still loved him. Even after everything.

I have something to tell you. Meet at the boats 2 mora?

Love Divided

When we'd first started going out we always used to talk about taking a boat out, but somehow we'd never got around to it. It didn't exactly feel like the best time to be going boating, but I didn't have the energy to think of somewhere else.

And maybe, just maybe, Mally had something good to tell me, for once. Maybe he was going to apologise for ignoring me by whisking me off for a glamorous holiday . . . Or maybe he was going to dump me. Jesus, this was completely bloody mad.

When I arrived at the boats, Mally was waiting for me, even though I was early. At first we didn't have time to say much to each other – we were too busy choosing a boat and sorting everything out with the guy who worked there. Then I got in, wobbling awkwardly and holding on to Mally's hand.

We sat down and Mally started rowing and I looked at him for the first time. His face was tilted downwards and his hair flopped over one eye the way it always did.

Why did he still have to be so ridiculously beautiful?

My heart was stomping around like a wild animal in my chest; I was sure Mally would have heard it if the water had not been so loud. It slipped and slapped the side of our little boat and made our silence not seem so obvious.

Calm down, Lucy. He's only a boy.

After a few pulls on the oars Mally said, 'Lucy. Look, I'm sorry. I know I've been avoiding you.'

Even though I'd rehearsed our conversation a thousand times, when I opened my mouth my words came out strange and stilted, as if I was still in one of my dreams. 'You have been avoiding me,' I said. 'Why?'

'I've been a mess. The whole Cambridge thing.' Mally was now looking somewhere past my left ear. I could see the muscles on his arm flex and relax as he worked the oars.

'What are you going to do?'

'What do you mean?'

'About Cambridge.'

'Oh. It turns out I only failed one module, in economics. So I'm going to retake it, next summer probably. Then I'll reapply. I'll have to have a year off though, which wasn't part of the plan.'

A year off – that might mean Mally would still be around and we could be together . . . Was that what he was going to tell me?

I waited.

'Which brings me to the news I have,' Mally said. He still wouldn't look at me. 'I'm really sorry – God, why am I saying I'm sorry? What I mean is that I'm excited – and – this is the thing.'

Mally took a breath and finally looked at me. God, those eyes! They still had the power to send an electric shock straight to my heart.

'I've decided to go to Bangladesh for part of my year off.'

I opened my mouth, then closed it again. 'Oh,' I said.

'It'll look good on my CV and, well, I might have the chance to do some good.' Mally spoke hurriedly, as if he was afraid I was going to interrupt him. 'I'm going to my family's village. There's a charity there that sets up schools for kids who've been flooded out of their homes.'

'Right.' I hadn't really taken anything in, except that Mally was planning to spend the next year fifteen million miles away. 'Is that . . . is that what you were going to tell me? Is that why you wanted to meet?'

'Yes. I'm sorry, I know it's probably not what you wanted to hear, but, you know, it's an amazing opportunity.'

So he wasn't going to dump me. But he was going halfway round the world without me. I wanted to laugh and cry at the same time.

'How long? How long are you going for?'

'Six months.'

'*Six months!*' That was longer than we'd been going out for.

'They don't really do placements for less than that. It's about making the most out of the experience and well . . .' Mally trailed off.

What about my experience! Have you even, for one moment, thought of me in all of this? I don't think I've ever felt as lonely as I did in that moment, with the boy I loved most in the world sitting right beside me.

'I know, it's all a bit of a shock, Lucy. It is to me too. I'm sorry. You know I love you, right?'

'When are you going?'

'Next week.'

This was all too much to take in. I started to cry. 'How can you do this to me? I love you so much. I thought . . . I thought we were for real.' I was sounding totally desperate but I didn't care.

'We *are* for real, sweetheart. I've never felt for anyone else half what I've felt for you. It's just that, I don't know, there are so many other things going on in my life right now. It's difficult for me to, to, focus entirely on this relationship.'

It wasn't difficult for me. It was all I did, focus on Mally. I was a Mally expert.

Mally leaned forward and very gently wiped a tear from my cheek. 'I've got to do things with my life. I can't just hang around Redworth for a year, waiting for something to happen.'

But that was exactly what he was asking me to do. '*I'm* in Redworth. Doesn't that mean anything?'

'Of course it does. You'll always be my Lucy Luce.' Mally gave me a little smile. He looked like a god sitting there in the sunshine. Beautiful. And completely out of reach.

'Why didn't you call me this whole week? Didn't you . . . didn't you think I might like to know about all this, you know, a bit sooner?'

'I know. You're completely right. I was really busy organising everything, then I didn't want to tell you and then not go.'

'Why? Because you thought I'd get hysterical?'

'No, because I didn't want to hurt you.'

'You are hurting me.' I suddenly thought of Quin, and how I hadn't been able to be honest with him and only hurt him more. Maybe Mally was doing the same. 'You know, when you didn't reply to any of my messages I walked all over town looking for you. I even walked by your house. Then I just gave up and sat at home. I haven't eaten. I haven't seen anyone. I've been in so much pain: it's like my leg's been cut off or something. I actually don't know what to do.'

Mally shifted on his seat. 'I'm sorry . . . I guess I kept thinking I'd call, then somehow I couldn't face it.'

'But *why*?'

'I've been thinking about this. I know it's completely unreasonable but I was angry at you. You kept calling me and I just wanted to be left alone. I guess I needed to lick my wounds.'

'But I just wanted to help!' I felt sick. All this time I'd been so worried but Mally had been *avoiding me*. I felt like a bug he'd just squashed against the windscreen.

'I know that. But I didn't need your help.' Mally saw the look on my face. 'I'm sorry, Luce, that sounds mean. What I'm trying to say is that there was nothing you could do. What were you going to do? Help me resit my exam?'

'I meant, help you *emotionally*,' I said, gripping on to the side of the boat. So it wasn't to do with his dad at all. This was like a nightmare. 'I could have been there for you. That's what couples do.'

'Right,' said Mally. 'I know. But I'd put so much stock on getting into Cambridge. When I didn't, I just wanted to be by myself. To process it all. I've had to rearrange the whole of next year and it's been quite difficult.'

'*Quite difficult*?' I shouted. 'WHAT ABOUT ME?!'

How had this happened? How had my beautiful Mally, who I could confide everything in, the only one who had understood me in the entire world, turned into this? Mum had been right. I would have turned to Mally at the first sign of trouble. *Why didn't he want to do the same?*

I still loved him. I loved him more than ever. Maybe because I knew I couldn't have him, at least not in the way I wanted him. If only he had been willing to put just a little bit of his life on hold for me. Like when Socks died. Or even if he'd called me in pieces after his results. And now he was going away and I would be left here. Alone. I didn't know how I was going to deal with it.

'I don't see how this is going to work,' I said, more to myself than to him. 'If you can't be there for me when we live a couple of streets away, how is it going to be when you're on the other side of the world?'

'We can write. Email.' Mally smiled but I looked away from him. He was too painful to look at.

'Yeah, I can just imagine checking the computer every five minutes and you never emailing because you're too busy saving the world.'

'What are you saying, Lucy?'

'I'm saying . . .' I gave a gulp. 'I'm saying that we should split up.'

Saying those words tore my heart out of my chest all over again.

I couldn't bear the thought of my life without Mally.

I had expected Mally to react angrily, to disagree. But instead he reached forward and put his arms around me – which was far worse. 'I'm sorry. I . . . don't know what to say.'

Say you love me! Say you won't let it happen! I thought desperately. *I'd made a mistake – I didn't mean it!*

But neither of us spoke. I remember reading somewhere that to be able not to speak to someone is a sign of true intimacy. Fat lot of use that was now.

'I'm sorry, Lucy. You're my first love. My best love. You know that, right? It's just the timing that sucked . . .'

Oh God! He was actually agreeing with me. What the hell had I done?'

'So . . . it's . . . we're . . . finished?'

Mally looked at the bottom of the boat. 'I really admire you for doing this. It hurts like hell, but . . . I think you're right. I'm probably not at a place where I can commit right now.' He looked up helplessly. 'I love you.'

'I love you.'

I started to cry.

Mally leaned forward and kissed me. His lips felt warm and dry.

But why couldn't he love me as much as I loved him?

I wished this kiss could last for ever. But it ended, like everything did.

'We should probably go,' I said. Suddenly I felt angry. 'A part of me hates you, you know. I would have done anything for you.'

'Lucy, you're right, you have every reason —'

'Stop being so bloody rational!' I shot back. 'Don't you . . . you're just sitting there, when you're going to Bangladesh any second.'

'I have to live my life!'

'Yes, without me!'

'Don't make this harder than it already is. I might look OK to you Lucy, but I'm not.'

'You're doing a whole lot better than me,' I said.

Mally picked up the oars and began to row. I couldn't look at Mally's face. Instead I fixed on the silver studs in his belt and the shift of his T-shirt as he rowed, willing myself not to fall apart.

We were back. I started to cry again. Mally put his oars up and cupped my face with both his hands. 'You know there will always be a part of me that loves you. You're the most wonderful person I've ever met. I know you'll do really well. Be a famous fashion designer!' Mally smiled awkwardly. I hated the way he was envisioning my life without him. 'Goodbye, sweetheart.'

I couldn't speak. There was nothing left to say in any case. I just struggled out of the boat in a blur and ran and ran until I knew that even if I turned around, Mally would not be there.

Chapter 13

♥

Whenever anyone asked me how I was I said, 'Welcome to Lucy's Wonderful World of Pain. Come inside, if you dare!' I had to make a joke out of it; I was seriously beginning to suspect that, if I didn't, none of my friends would call me any more. I was talking all their ears off.

The problem was that every thought led back to Mally.

The whole town, for a start. Then things as random as the summer (we had been together in it), anything to do with rivers or boats, black jeans, sad songs, the whole Indian subcontinent including food, people, global warming, floods. Then there were Muslims, cappuccinos, double-decker buses, London. And all that was only a tiny part of what reminded me of him. You can see how I made for pretty boring company.

A few days after the split I became convinced that I'd done the wrong thing, that Mally didn't want to break up, that I should call him RIGHT NOW and beg him to take me back. It was only Mum hiding all the phones in the house that stopped me. I wrote him a thousand emails and sat there with my mouse on the *send* button. I looked him up on MySpace and Bebo. I could see when he was online and that made him feel so close, just a touch away. I imagined Mally sitting at his computer, completely fine. And there was me, in pieces.

I imagined him choosing what clothes to pack, what he'd put on his iPod for the journey. I wished I could make him a going-away playlist. I couldn't believe that he was embarking on this whole adventure without me. I couldn't believe we turned out to be two separate people after all, when all along I had thought we were two halves of one whole.

I always used to think that you fell in love and that was it, happily ever after. But now I know it's more complicated than that. Mally had loved me, but the timing was all wrong. His dad didn't split us up, but he made things harder.

If we'd met later, would we have had a chance? What if I'd met Mr Right at the wrong time?

I'll never know, and to think like that will only drive me insane.

Mum was being amazing. She came home from work early and sat with me and I literally cried on her shoulder.

'You know, you think this is all about Mally not being

ready,' she said. 'But have you thought about things from your own perspective? I know you feel grown-up but you've still got so much of your life to live. Were you really ready to settle down, for ever and ever, with one man? I know you think you were. But in a few months' time, you'll be at a party, I bet you, and you'll be having fun again. You've got the rest of your life ahead of you!'

But that was what I was afraid of. The rest of my Mally-less life.

'I hope you're right,' I said.

'I am. I'm bigger and older and uglier than you. I have to be right.'

Even Herbie was being sweet: he gave me ownership of the remote control. He even did my share of the chores. But the best thing was that Ehsan had started showing up again. Herbie seemed really pleased – I guess Ehsan had been his best friend. And Herbie being a nerd, doesn't make friends that easily.

And then there was Rachel. Apart from my family, Rachel was the only one that I could talk to without worrying about getting boring. Rachel was single now – she said after Ian she had realised she had to get to know herself before she could get to know anyone else. Which meant we were there for each other 24/7. I phoned her late at night from my bedroom and just talked and talked until my throat got dry. Occasionally we even talked about things other than boys – things like hair, make-up, saving the world. When that happened I stopped thinking about Mally for whole minutes at a time and I realised that, just for that moment, I felt lighter. It had all got so heavy with Mally and so complicated. With Rachel I could just be a girl again – or, as Mum would have said, a woman.

I had to keep busy to stop myself going mad. I didn't feel much like shopping or going out, so at long last I decided to redecorate my room. The little girl who had mooned over posters of boy bands just wasn't me any more. On one of my trips to the second-hand shop I'd found this amazing tailor's dummy, which I'd stuck in the garage. Now I moved it upstairs. The dummy would be good for my new designs – I was thinking I might branch out into jackets. On the wall I pinned up a gorgeous piece of fabric I'd found in Mum's wardrobe – a really bold Seventies pattern. I only had two posters up now. One was of Jeff Buckley swooning over a microphone – OK, I know he's a boy, and he was in a band, but it's completely different from a *boy band*, trust me. The other poster was an amazing picture of the earth taken from outer space. It was there to remind me that the earth is precious and that it's my home and that I share it with everyone else, even Mally, even in Bangladesh. And then I collected together all the precious things from our relationship: the Coke can ring, the CD Mally burned for me, a flower Mally had given me that I'd pressed between the pages of a book and the photo he'd taken of us on the bus in London. I put them in a beautiful box that sat on my desk and I turned the key. I'd keep the key under my pillow until I was ready to let it go.

I was glad I'd got round to redecorating at last. I felt like I finally knew what I wanted in my room, like I finally knew myself.

Even so, I couldn't sleep well that week. I was still dreaming of Mally only to wake up and realise we'd split up. So I put off going to bed. It was on one of those nights that I thought I heard something – or someone – outside on the street. Probably a fox – they were always going through our bins. But I listened again. It was too quiet and too deliberate for a fox.

Immediately my thoughts flew to Mally.

I ran to the window and tore back the curtain.

Nothing.

But . . . I was *sure* I heard something.

I ran downstairs, opened the front door and peered out into the street. A dark figure, the same height as Mally, was halfway down it, walking fast. Whoever it was obviously did not want to stop and talk. On my way back indoors my foot stumbled on something. A stone, and under the stone, a letter.

It *had* been Mally!

I picked them both up and ran back upstairs. But it wasn't until I was snuggled up in bed that I began to read. I wanted to savour every last word.

My Darling Lucy,

As I'm writing this I'm hoping that I'll have a chance to see you tonight for the last time. Then again, if I do see you, I don't know that I'll be able to handle it.

You were incredibly brave to end it and I'll always admire you for it. I couldn't. You did the right thing, sweetheart. I'm so incredibly sorry if I've caused you pain.

I probably don't have the right to ask you to think of me in Bangladesh but I know I'll be thinking of you, every evening at six o' clock. I'll look up into the stars and I'll feel better because I'll know they're the same stars that you're underneath too.

I've left you something. I found the pebble on the bank when I was returning the boat. It looked so beautiful, the flecks of silver in it reminded me of the flecks in your eyes.

You're the only pebble on the beach worth anything to me.

Mally x

I folded up the paper carefully and put it under my pillow. Mally was right, the stone was beautiful. I turned it in the light; the little flecks in it glinted and shone like stars. It was perfectly oval and snug in the palm of my hand. I turned it over – there was writing. Mally had had it engraved: *To one in a million. M.*

I turned off the light with the pebble still in my hand. I was really tired and I had a feeling I'd sleep better tonight than I had in ages.

☆

www.piccadillypress.co.uk

☆ The latest news on forthcoming books

☆ Chapter previews

☆ Author biographies

☆ Fun quizzes

☆ Reader reviews

☆ Competitions and fab prizes

☆ Book features and cool downloads

☆ And much, much more . . .

Log on and check it out!

Piccadilly Press

☆